D1516443

ALSO BY

AMARA LAKHOUS

Clash of Civilizations Over an Elevator in Piazza Vittorio

Divorce Islamic Style

Dispute Over a Very Italian Piglet

THE PRANK
OF THE GOOD
LITTLE VIRGIN
OF VIA ORMEA

Amara Lakhous

THE PRANK
OF THE GOOD
LITTLE VIRGIN
OF VIA ORMEA

Translated from the Italian
by Antony Shugaar

Europa
editions

Europa Editions
214 West 29th Street
New York, N.Y. 10001
www.europaeditions.com
info@europaeditions.com

Translation by Antony Shugaar
Original title: *La zingarata della verginella di Via Ormea*
Translation copyright © 2016 by Europa Editions

Library of Congress Cataloging in Publication Data is available
ISBN 978-1-60945-309-1

Lakhous, Amara
The Prank of the Good Little Virgin of Via Ormea

Book design by Emanuele Ragnisco
www.mekkanografici.com

Cover illustration by Chiara Carrer

Prepress by Grafica Punto Print – Rome

Printed in the USA

To two generous friends:
Vincenzo Consolo (1933-2012)
and Armando Gnisci

"There has never been since New-York was founded
so low and ignorant a class among the immigrants
who poured in here as the Italians. [...] They
become the scavengers of our streets, their children
grow up in filthy cellars, packed with rags and bones,
or in crowded attics, where many families lodge
together, and then are sent out into the streets to
make money by the street trades."
The New York Times, March 5, 1882

A wise man laughs when he can.
He knows very well that there will be much
to cry about in life.
ROMA PROVERB

CONTENTS

THE PRANK
OF THE GOOD
LITTLE VIRGIN
OF VIA ORMEA

CHAPTER ONE
It's a funeral, but no one died

There's no finer wine to toast with than a good Nebbiolo. "Long live Turin, home to invention and creativity," says Tania, amused, as she lifts her glass. We're sitting on the outdoor terrace of the Baby Bottle, the club in the San Salvario district run by my friends Paola and Sergio. The atmosphere is agreeable. We're enjoying this first dinner—or actually, this *apericena*, a combination of *aperitivo*, a before-dinner drink, and *cena*, dinner—of spring. In other parts of Italy they call it a happy hour, but that's not the same thing. Around here it starts at 6:30 and continues late into the night. It costs 5 or 6 euros and you can eat as much you want, choosing among the numerous pasta courses, entrées, and desserts. Plus they give you a free draft beer or glass of wine. Not bad, right? These days, with the recession and all, we have to tighten our belts.

"We must rediscover the virtues of frugality; even fasting can help families in dire economic straits make ends meet." This isn't something some economist from Harvard or Cambridge said; these are the words of none other than Aunt Quiz in person, my next-door neighbor as well as my mother's own hired spy. What Aunt Quiz says is taken seriously and considered all but sacred, at least here in San Salvario. She's an extraordinary housewife, with extensive experience of life and television. They don't call her Quiz for nothing. She earned that nickname fair and square. She knows exactly how to spend money and, most importantly, how to scrimp and save and the best way to keep deceitful shopkeepers from ripping you off. Self-styled home economics experts, the ones who bullshit their way from one television talk show to another, have nothing on her. She, at least, is a serious person.

The *apericena* can save you a load of trouble, for instance the trouble of cooking. Not everyone likes donning the apron and spending hours making this dish or that. Patience is a rare virtue, one that not everyone possesses. Now, the big news that fills us with joy and pride is this: It would seem that the *apericena* was invented right here at home in Turin (anyone who says Milan or Rome is nothing but a liar, a real son of a bitch). To be perfectly straight with you, yours truly can neither confirm nor deny. You'd need to consult an expert on the matter.

My generic observations on the subject pique Tania's curiosity. She listens to me with interest and admiration. Some of you may wonder why. I can't say with any real precision. Maybe it's because I'm a super-smart guy, or else it's just that she's crazy about me. Option number two is sure to piss off all those assholes who have no love for Enzo Laganà and who can't stand seeing him arm in arm with a beautiful Finnish babe, a genuine blonde. Who would have bet on our becoming a couple when we first met five years ago here in Turin? No one. Much less my mother. But Tania has held up famously, racking up a fantastic record, no less an achievement than six years as a couple. The secret? It remains a secret. I'm not saying that because I want to keep it to myself, but quite simply because I still don't know.

To get back to our toast. The *apericena* is one of the great new developments of the past few years. Tania really likes to be part of new trends, especially right at the beginning when no one but scattered dreamers, creatives, visionaries, and madmen believe in them. Unfortunately, as we know, innocence, authenticity, and purity are short-lived, extremely so. Soon enough, fashion is held hostage by marketing, consumerism,

and the rest of the usual suspects. It turns into a mass phenomenon. All you're left with at that point is one slim hope:
that the new fashion will as soon as possible go completely *out*
of fashion.

Talking with Tania, eating good food, and drinking good
wine. What more could I ask? Happiness consists of simple
untroubled moments like these. It's a pleasure to wait, and
we're waiting for the start of my Moroccan friend Samir's
show; his stage name is Sam. The young man is on the
upswing, he's making great strides in the musical world. In just
a few weeks, he's scheduled to record his second CD. Right
now he's enjoying the spotlight. He's booked shows not only in
Italy, but in other European countries as well. He really is a
genius, he seems to know how to play any instrument he lays
his hands on. Sooner or later he'll make it big. It's just a matter of time and, of course, luck.

I tell Tania the latest news about Sam. There are substantial
changes coming down the pike. He's just come back from
Morocco where he spent a month with his family. He hadn't
been home for many years. It shook something loose inside
him. Yours truly has a real gift for observing people and things.
A love for details is the very basis of the journalist's profession.
Of course I feel a need to point out that my weakness for
details has nothing to do with the kind of morbid curiosity on
which reality television is predicated. The very thought makes
me want to throw up. Observing Sam, I've picked up on a few
new wrinkles. The worrisome thing is that he's gotten some
very strange ideas into his head—getting married, for example.
It's a safe bet that the bride-to-be will be a Moroccan girl, born
and bred. In other words, the proverbial girl next door. Better
to stick with the tried and true. Marriage is risky business,
worse than playing the stock market. My personal crusade
against holy matrimony is a fight to the finish; we've been at
war for years now. Will we finally make peace someday?

"What's so strange about wanting to start a family?" Tania breaks in.

"Can you see Sam as a family man? Please, don't make me laugh."

"Why not? I don't understand you."

"Sam is an artist."

"So what? Is there some law against artists getting married and having children?"

"What I'm trying to say is that Sam can barely even look after himself."

"So you think he's not ready, is that it?"

"Exactly."

"No one's ever ready, but people learn over time by doing things, instead of letting the fear of making a mistake stop them."

Tania's words seem to come directly from my mother's mouth. Is that a coincidence, or is there something more to this? Is a conspiracy being hatched against me? This strikes me as a perfectly reasonable question.

"The risk is that someone will get hurt," I retort.

"What about you? Do you feel ready?"

"What does this have to do with me? We're talking about Sam!" I cut her off.

I react like a boxer who barely manages to dodge a power-ful left hook. For a moment, I feel as if I've glimpsed Mike Tyson's angry, menacing glare. I suddenly feel the urge to hide my face and throw up my guard. The truth is, I don't love talk-ing about these kinds of things. These kinds of conversations are not exactly my bread and butter. It's in my best interest to give all talk of marriage, having kids, becoming a husband, son-in-law, father, grandfather, etc., a wide berth. My sainted mother is already doing a first-rate job discussing all these things. She's the specialist.

So I avoid letting myself be led by the nose like some bored donkey and I try to keep sight of the real topic of conversation: that asshole Sam. He arrived at the idea of fathering a family step by step. He started out by sending coded messages (what a pain in the ass), such as: "Sooner or later you've got to screw your head on straight," "The single life is a shitty one," and "It's time to grow up." That last piece of bullshit is the one I hate most. What is "It's time to grow up" supposed to mean, anyway? I don't think you can schedule personal growth. How the hell are you supposed to do that? You just grow, that's all there is to it. Which is to say that as you get older you accumulate experience, that is, mistakes. If you've got any sense, you'll stop fucking the same things up over and over, and if you don't, you'll just keep repeating the same script and at the end of the day you'll be taking it up the you-know-what.

After a while, good old Sam made an impressive qualitative leap, placing himself, if you can believe it, in the shoes of a genuine father: "I still can't wrap my mind around the idea of letting some boy come into my home and fuck my daughter just because he happens to be this month's boyfriend!" And now we see the Muslim lurking beneath the surface, gaining the upper hand. Fucking hell, he's worried about a daughter who hasn't even been born yet. If anyone's looking for the dictionary definition of mental masturbation, here we have it. I decide that Sam and his bullshit can go to hell in the same handbasket, and I change the subject.

"You're finally going to discover the mountains of Piedmont," I say to Tania with a smile as I stroke her hair.

"I can't wait. I need to recover from all those trips I took without you."

"It's not eay to win your forgiveness."

"Maybe you should put in a little more effort."

"I'll give it my all."

Guys, here I'm going to have to engage in some serious self-criticism. Lately, I've been losing points. I'll admit I've lost my well-known verve, my eagerness to discover new places—in short, my thirst for adventure. Tania has every right to scold me for my laziness. I've turned down plenty of her invitations and suggestions that we go on trips. It's time for me to shake the dust off, get up and at it again. A week in the mountains will do me good. It's a great way to get started again, to get back to the good old days.

It was Tania who arranged everything. It's nice to relax and let someone else take the wheel, but you can't make a habit of it. Otherwise you run the risk of winding up like those donkeys. I'm a young man who's pretty jealous of my independence and I absolutely refuse to give up my freedom. If there's one advantage to being single or, perhaps I should say, to being an eligible bachelor (I just love this expression), it's that I can live on my own without worrying about making ends meet or similar pains in the ass—and believe me, the list goes on and on.

Now, my personal life is a little unusual. Tania and I are neither single nor married. We see each other whenever we feel like it and we indulge in days of passion. She's still a European rep for Nokia, and I live in Turin full-time. We meet up pretty frequently in one European city or another. My sister, who lives in Detroit with her husband and my two little nephews, has no doubts: "Your problem, dear brother, isn't getting married; it's power." Her theory is quite simple: Getting married is like going into business with someone. You have to renounce the concept of absolute power and start living with compromises. So in my case, a wife (*mogliera* is the Calabrian word that my mother uses) is some sort of threat to my power and to my categorical rejection of the logic of compromise. I've retorted plenty of times, and my line is always the same: "What does power have to do with any of this? The crux of the matter is my wholly legitimate right to do what I please with my life." You can't really get much clearer than that.

Unfortunately the best things in life don't last long. You always have to take into account the likelihood of rude surprises. And in fact the blessed peace and Tania's delightful company are spoiled by an unexpected arrival: Mario Bellezza, the unrivaled chief of the "Masters of Our Own Home" neighborhood committee, bursts onto the scene. He retired from his day job a few years ago after a lifetime at Fiat. Instead of spending time with his grandchildren or going back to his old village in Calabria to enjoy the sunshine and good food, he's decided to spoil his life and the lives of us poor residents of San Salvario. He's constantly setting up new citizens' committees, all of which have the same main goal: to harrass immigrants.

As usual, Bellezza is panting thanks to his obesity. His gut is completely out of control. I even wonder whether there's still any point in referring to it as a gut. Wouldn't it make more sense to call things by their real names and finally trot out the term "beer belly"? Now there's a fine nickname: Beerbelly. Bellezza the Beerbelly, not Bellezza the fattie. Quite original. When you drink that much beer you have to pay the tab eventually, my good man.

Bellezza is upset; it looks like storm clouds on the horizon. He comes over to our table and takes a seat with no regard for even the most basic rules of etiquette, which require asking permission and saying hello. It wouldn't hurt to throw in a couple of nicely turned phrases, especially in the presence of a woman. Sad to say, there's nothing to be done about him. The man would need to be completely retrained. As far as I'm concerned, I wouldn't bet one red cent on the success of even that operation. When you're dealing with a lost cause, you have to know when to give up. I've known him since I was born; he worked with my father. I've personally witnessed both the growth of his gut and the degeneration of his political beliefs. He's slid from the left wing to the right without even noticing.

"Enzo! Here you are, at last! I've been looking everywhere for you. I even went to your paper's newsroom."

"Do you want a glass of water?" I ask in a bid to calm him down.

"I want a large beer, ice-cold."

"Well then, things must be serious. What's happened?"

"A fine mess, Enzo. The gypsies have raped a young girl from the neighborhood."

"The gypsies! *All* the gypsies?" I ask, trying to figure out what he's saying.

"No, two Roma twins."

"Where and when?"

There was no doubt about it. I couldn't go wrong. Only beer could soothe his nerves. Bellezza is possessed of an outstanding verbal prowess. Once he starts talking, no one can stop him. His anecdotes are rich in detail, backstory, parenthetical asides, footnotes, cross-references, and most of all, goddamned commentary. Now, what's essential to every good story is the lead-in. Where to begin? Bellezza can't seem to find the key to the ignition. The car won't turn over and there seems to be no way to give it a jump start. He always makes the same damn mistake: He gets lost in the preliminaries. Which is a tremendous problem for yours truly. What can we do about it? I've never been blessed with the virtue of patience. And Tania's presence onstage hardly helps matters. Talking about rape in a woman's presence is even more complicated. You have to employ tact. And it's truly pointless to ask Bellezza alias Beerbelly to choose his words judiciously. It's mission impossible.

I try to help out. I ask him to start with the concrete facts and then to proceed from there to the commentary and the lessons to be drawn. After a number of false starts we finally succeed. It's not that complicated when you start with the central deed, or rather misdeed: Two hours ago a young

Italian girl was raped by twin Roma brothers. How did it happen? And above all, where did it happen? This time Bellezza disappoints, providing only the scantiest of information. His narrative is in fact a bare-bones account that can be summarized in just a few words: This afternoon, after school, Virginia (that's the name of the fifteen-year-old rape victim) went to the volunteer association "Together," on Corso Marconi in the San Salvario neighborhood, where she helped local schoolchildren with their homework, just as she does every week. Apparently she knew her attackers. The two Roma boys sexually assaulted her in the association building, but where exactly? In the bathroom? There are no answers, only conjectures. Bellezza gradually begins to warm to his theme. The ice-cold beer starts to take effect. He's not about to miss an opportunity to put two and two together, obliging us to listen to an old and familiar record: "We can't let things go on like this. We've hit rock bottom! What could be worse than the gang rape of a young girl just a stone's throw from her home, and right under our noses?" There's more: "Jesus fucking Christ, do we or do we not have the right to be the masters of our own homes?"

Bellezza rediscovers his famous moxie: "It's time to say we've had it with the gypsies and the immigrants, it's time to get them the hell out from underfoot," he says, piling it on. Tania emerges from her silence and asks him where the young girl is now. This time Beerbelly has an answer: She's gone back home after being examined by a physician at the hospital. There can be no doubt about the rape; unfortunately Virginia has lost her virginity. As for filing a report with the police, Bellezza doesn't put much stock in that.

"What good would that do?" he asks, raising his voice.

"Going to the police is the best solution," Tania puts in.

"Unfortunately we don't live in Sweden here." Bellezza is trying to refer the country of Tania's birth, but he gets it wrong.

The most famous Italian theorem strikes again: All blondes are Swedish.

"There are no alternatives to the authorities," I agree.

"That's not true; in fact we have a very nice alternative indeed," Bellezza assures me.

"Oh, we do, do we? What, exactly?" I ask.

And off he goes with the greatest undertaking ever conceived in the San Salvario neighborhood. Bellezza explains to us that at this point all self-respecting citizens feel betrayed and abandoned by public institutions. There's only one solution: to roll up our sleeves. To stand on our own two feet. What does that mean? Starting our own security patrols. An old fixation. Self-defense is a basic right of every human being. Bellezza has more faith in the citizenry and the mass media than in the police and the Carabinieri put together. And that's why he has such high hopes for me, and for the hard-hitting article he wants me to write. Virginia's rape needs to become the national—no, wait, European; better yet, global—cause. "Those bastard gypsies won't get off easy this time. You can count on it. We need to expel them not only from Italy, but from the whole of Europe."

I don't even have time to ask him where he plans to send them before my cell phone rings. It's my managing editor, Angelo Maritani. He informs me of a news agency report that's just hit the wires about the rape of fifteen-year-old Italian girl by a "pack of gypsies" in San Salvario. So the two Roma boys have already turned into a pack? I tell him I know all about it. How could I let news like that get past me? If I'm not up-to-date on everything that's happening in my neighborhood, what good am I as a crime reporter? I impress Maritani for a couple of reasons. First, I reel off all the information Bellezza gave me without forgetting a thing. After years of reporting, I've learned how to stretch the broth and add a little spice to the news. Second, yours truly is already aware of the case in question, which is a huge advantage in our line of work: A good reporter on the crime beat needs to have excellent radar, a nose for the story. It's not about having second sight or a sixth sense; it's more about knowing how to be in the right place at the right time. In other words it's not always a matter of dumb luck, it takes a little something extra. Good luck is certainly welcome, but you need to be agile and know how to bolt in the right direction.

To put a quick end to this phone call with Maritani, I tell him that I'm heading straight over to the victim's home. He urges me to keep him posted in real time. The editor in chief, Salvini himself, is taking an interest in the case. That Salvini: He's a purebred hunting hound, not a bone escapes him.

I leave Tania at the Baby Bottle to enjoy Sam's show and ask Bellezza to take me to the young rape victim's home.

* * *

It looks like a genuine funeral. All that's missing is a hearse and the funeral home attendants dressed in black. That's what I thought to myself at the young girl's parents' apartment, on Via Ormea. Bellezza clears a path authoritatively, pushing through a line of people crowding both the stairs and the front door of the second-story apartment. Who are all these people? What are they doing here? Maybe they're relatives, or friends, or just rubberneckers who want a preview of the show that the mass media are already mounting, on television first and foremost. I find myself catapulted to the center of the living room. They push me to a seat next to the young girl's grandmother, who weeps as she obsessively repeats the same monotonous dirge: "They've destroyed the flower of my life! Holy Virgin Mary, mother of our Jesus, why didn't You protect my little girl?" I ask about Virginia and they tell me that she's shut up in her bedroom, in her mother's arms. A guy in his early forties comes over, his eyes welling with tears. Bellezza steps aside to make way for him. This is the father of the victim. We know each other. His name is Mauro Ferreri. We went to all the same schools in San Salvario. He must be a couple of years older than me. To be the father of a teenage girl he must have married young, no doubt about it. He has a cigarette in one hand, but he doesn't light it, he just keeps staring at it. He looks like an ex-smoker on the verge of falling off the wagon.

"Thanks for coming, Enzo."

"The very least I could do," I reply.

"What are we supposed to do?" he adds, disconsolate, throwing both arms up into the air.

"I'm so sorry, Mauro. How is your daughter?"

"She's traumatized. I don't know how we're ever going to get past this disaster."

"You'll see, you'll survive."

You'll survive! Such certainty, such conviction. Good job, Enzo. They sound like the words that might come out of a priest's mouth. How on earth did I come up with them? I have to admit that I hate this kind of situation. I feel incompetent, out of place. It's like asking my idol, Michel Platini, a midfielder, to play goalie. I'm no good playing the part of the consoler. I can never find the right words and I can't stand the awkward silences. To pry myself out of this uncomfortable situation I reach into my jacket and pull out my pen and my notebook. Better to go for camouflage. I start jotting down a few notes.

I explain to Mauro that I'm not here out of curiosity, but to do my job. I take advantage of the chance to make clear that I'm not just some unscrupulous jackal on the hunt for scoops and sensationalist gossip. Far from it. I tell him that I understand the situation completely. I certainly hope I'm not intruding, but I'd like to have some more information to help me write my article. Unfortunately Mauro reels off practically the same version as Bellezza. I push him to answer at least a couple of questions: Did Virginia know her attackers? Exactly where did the misdeed take place? No answer. He tells me that the details won't do anyone any good. The only important fact is that his baby girl was brutally raped by a gang of feral animals.

Suddenly the grandmother starts up a moving plea to the Madonna. Her lamentations grow progressively louder. So the first impression I had when I came in turns out to be correct: What I'm attending here is a funeral, but no one is dead. Where's the corpse? Come to think of it, the corpse that the grandmother is weeping over does exist, and how: her virginity, may it rest in peace.

A skinny kid comes over and wraps his arms around the old woman. He tries to make her stop, without success. We watch the conversation between the two, in silence.

"Please, Grandma, stop crying."

"Oh, Giuliano, my boy. There's nothing we can do anymore."

"The rapists aren't going to get away with it. They need to pay for what they've done."

"You're right. We need to react forcefully," Bellezza puts in.

"Fucking gypsies," adds Giuliano, with tears in his eyes.

Now there are two of them crying. Mauro explains that the boy is his nephew. To Virginia he's like a brother, the two of them grew up together. He's blinded by rage and grief. He wants to take revenge. Virginia is the sister he never had, they love each other so much.

Not satisfied with this version of the facts, I play a very delicate card in an attempt to dig up more details. Let's hope it works out. I turn to the father.

"Can I talk to Virginia?"

"I'm sorry, Enzo. My daughter is a wreck."

"I promise that I won't take much of her time."

"Leave us in peace. Jackals from the press are the last thing we need," says the cousin, addressing me.

"I'm here to do my work. If I'm bothering anyone I'm happy to leave right away," I try to explain.

"Virginia isn't talking with anyone, is that clear?" the cousin reiterates.

"Calm down, Giuliano! Enzo is a friend," Bellezza breaks in.

"We don't need journalists and we don't need the police. We can take revenge for ourselves."

"You're looking for revenge? Well then, good luck," I say, wishing him my best and putting an end to the discussion.

The cousin's reaction is understandable, I shouldn't take it the wrong way. I'd do the same thing in his place. Rape is a horrible thing. It affects not merely the victim, but the family as well. It's a collective trauma, a loss of security and trust in one's fellow man.

I decide to leave. Bellezza instead decides to stay to perform his duties as a resident of the neighborhood. At times like this, it's important to make people feel that they're not alone, that their friends are close. All the same, this is also a tempting opportunity—too good to be wasted—for Beerbelly to win new converts over to the battles his committee is waging. I don't have time to swing back by the Baby Bottle. I call Tania to tell her that I'm going to the paper and that we'll see each other later.

* * *

A crime reporter's work is very similar to that of a firefighter. People call both of us in times of emergency, and they expect us to do our jobs in a hurry. Still, there is one substantial difference: While the firefighters' job is to put out the fire, we reporters are asked to pour on the gasoline. It's a funny job we do, isn't it?

I get to the newsroom and head straight for my office. My colleague on the culture desk who shares the room with me isn't there. Even better, I won't have any distractions. I want to get Maritani the article as quick as I can so I can get back to the Baby Bottle and continue my evening out with Tania.

I sit down and start rereading my notes. The young girl volunteers for a Catholic association. She's an untroubled person. Why should she lie? Why should she falsely accuse two Roma? In the material I've gathered there's nothing pertinent except the fifteen-year-old girl's version as reported by her father and by Bellezza. I write a first draft and reread it. It's not doing the trick. I decide to rewrite it in the conditional; that strikes me as a good solution. I print out the second draft and take it to Maritani, who reads it carefully. As he often does when the story is a sensitive one, he prefers to talk it over with Salvini, to delegate the hottest decisions to him and then obey his orders. The one more or less sure thing is that my article will appear in the national edition and that the boss himself will decide on the headline. That's his big specialty, aside from his famous editorials and his television appearances. The phone call between the two men is over quickly. Salvini is the only one who talks, my poor managing editor does nothing but listen and agree. We all have our jobs to do. In certain situations, Maritani demonstrates a gift that I deeply admire: He goes straight to the heart of the matter without beating around the bush.

"The editor in chief is very happy with your piece; there's just one little thing you'll need to change."

"What's that?"

"Take it out of the conditional."

"I don't think we should. Except for the girl's version, we have no other confirmation."

"I know, but that's how the editor in chief wants it."

"I don't understand."

"He claims it would be unjust to cast doubt on the young woman's word."

"Why?"

"It's like raping her all over again."

"And what do you think, Angelo?"

Maritani doesn't respond; there are other things he'd rather talk about. He admits that he can't go against Salvini's wishes: "The hierarchy must be respected, otherwise we risk anarchy." He parrots our editor in chief's favorite slogan. The suspicion flickers in my mind that his words might be aimed at me. It's no secret that Laganà doesn't give a fuck about the hierarchy. I often think of this newsroom as not unlike a military base. We have a general who exercises absolute power, issuing orders left and right. Then there are those of intermediate rank like Maritani, who act as middlemen. At the bottom are the poor privates like yours truly, who are expected to do nothing but execute orders and obey. I'm extremely allergic to this way of doing things. I hate obedience. I don't like barracks, whether military or civilian. A civilian barracks! That's a fine metaphor to describe a newsroom.

I decide to put an end to my discussion with Maritani. What's the use? I have more interesting things to do. For instance, there's a beautiful blonde waiting for me in a bar in San Salvario. It's not very nice to leave her there all on her own, is it?

I walk past the Savings Bank where I used to work. It's been a year since I've set foot in this part of town. I have the strange sensation of being in a place that's at once familiar and unknown. I stay for a few minutes to watch and think. At a certain point, two of my former colleagues, Paolini and Stradini, appear. They're probably on their way to get their usual espressos. We worked in the same office for many years. They brush past me and look at me without reacting at all. By now, no one recognizes me; in fact, no one even sees me. I'm invisible. Which is a major advantage. Everyone actually thinks I'm dead, even if my corpse was never found. Well done, me, my secret plan is working brilliantly.

I look at the Savings Bank from the outside for quite a few minutes. I don't dare go in. They'd immediately kick me out; at the very least I'd stir up suspicions. What would a gypsy woman even be doing in a bank in the first place? I spent twenty years of my life in this building. Twenty years that are lost to me now. The best years of my life, from when I was twenty-five to when I was forty-five. And what do I have to show for it? Nothing. Maybe nothing isn't the right answer. I do have something to show for it: a few regrets, or actually a great many. I can't pretend otherwise. You can't buy time and you can't sell it. You can earn all the money you want but you can't redeem even a single minute that's gone by. We can only do our best to console ourselves by saying that the past is past and what matters is the present, or else that you shouldn't cry over spilt milk. Blessed consolation, and words of consolation in particular, doesn't cost a penny. Words . . . words . . . words . . . *Nihil est dictu facilius*, nothing is easier than talking.

Above and beyond words, luckily, there are facts. The fact is that I am now a brand-new person, with a new identity, a new life, and "a new point of view," as my boss at the branch office used to say at every meeting. I've never understood what these five words mean when they're put together like that. *A new point of view*! A slogan no better or worse than any other, good only for creating even more ambiguity and confusion.

I often find myself thinking back on my life. It seems to me that I've somehow been reincarnated. It's like living in someone else's body. I'm aware of a few things: For instance, my memory is still intact, my past hasn't been erased. No amnesia, no brain damage. Still, I can't say that the change has been strictly external, because I now dress as a gypsy woman and I behave like one too. After a year, I feel that something has changed inside me as well. I don't see the world the way I used to. The way I understand things has changed completely. Now that I think about it, the so-called "new point of view" is simply a matter of changing our perspective so that we can see reality in a different light. A little like a director who moves the camera and shoots the same scene, only from a different angle. Maybe that's the point. In other words, life is all in the way you stage things, a performance in which everyone plays a role. There are the good and the bad, the rich and the poor, the winners and the losers, and so on and so forth. To see life as a movie: It's a fine metaphor, not bad at all I have to say. There has never been a movie that didn't come to an end. *The End*. The real problem, though, is that the roles are handed out more or less at random and the performance can be interrupted with no advance warning. *Acta est fabula*, the show is over. Isn't death mankind's biggest plot twist?

I often think of reincarnation as a brilliant idea as far as overcoming death goes. I was attracted by Buddhism when I was at university. The deeper I got into the world of banks, the further away Buddhism moved. There is no place for the teachings of the Buddha in a bank. A bank is anti-Buddhism at its peak. Karma is persona non grata there. No competition can be allowed. A bank is a temple to one God and one God only: money. A very particular kind of monotheism, no two ways about it.

I invested all my energy into my career. I put work at the center of my existence. It's not easy for a woman to trade elbows with her male coworkers. Competing with people of privilege is daunting and risky. I fought for a good position. I worked hard. In part, I was successful. In part . . . and that's the point. A partial victory is never a victory, it's always a partial defeat.

Then the toy broke. There were lots of different reasons. The most important one was the clear understanding (I'd say it came a little late, but better late than never) that work isn't everything. There are other paths to take, other means by which to achieve happiness. The main thing is to make sure you don't blindfold yourself; to keep searching without ever giving up.

There's one fundamental rule in all business: Diversify, never place all your bets on a single product. That's because if it's unsuccessful, the loss is total. Concentrating on work alone was a mistake. If I wanted to make up for it, I had only two options: find a new and similar toy and carry the farce on ad infinitum, or else stop playing once and for all. I chose the second. I absolutely couldn't go on. I was drowning in depression, the deadliest sea that there is. Luckily, I managed to save myself in time.

* * *

I don't remember when I decided to start working at the bank. It was a dream or a plan carried out methodically and with determination. The one sure thing though is that my dreams have changed over the years. When I was small I wanted to become a clown and make people laugh. I was in love with Charlie Chaplin. Charlie Chaplin is the only one who can still make me laugh and cry at the same time. A true genius. His autobiography is one of my favorite books. He lived a life full of challenges. He became a very wealthy man after suffering from hunger in London, where he was born. His mother had mental problems and his father was a drunk. As an immigrant in the United States, he achieved success with his Tramp character after numerous failures. To me, he remains a formidable example of how willpower can make all the difference. I don't remember the name of the movie in which Chaplin plays an officer who falls in love with a beautiful gypsy smuggler named Carmen. Could I have been influenced by that movie in my decision to become a gypsy? Who can say.

Deep down, a clown is a child in a grown-up's body. And in fact, in *The Kid*, Charlie Chaplin's finest movie as far as I'm concerned, you can't figure out which one is the child and which the adult, the Tramp or the orphan. A clown is by definition the symbol of innocence. Here, perhaps, is the weak point that has plagued my life. I believe too strongly in innocence. I'm always in search of innocence. Unfortunately, the world is made up of other things, too: cruelty, bullying, treachery—the list is long. Bad people do everything they can to make us lose the best part of ourselves, that is, our humanity. And often they succeed, with the slightest of efforts.

I used to think that the world of clowns was perfect. You play, you have fun, you feel things, you cry, you joke. But as I grew older I realized that it actually wasn't. Perfection is my other bête noire. Clowns live and work in a big house known as the circus. A terrible environment where the animals exist in conditions of permanent captivity and are often beaten and mistreated. Obviously the audience looks on, indifferent to their suffering. I hate the circus because people's laughter comes at the cost of others' unhappiness. No compassion. No solidarity. Total indifference reigns supreme. Perhaps the clown is someone who cries and denounces that situation.

The bank, too, is like a circus, but I'd say it's even more atrocious: Instead of animals, there are human beings in flesh and blood. One laughs while the other weeps. One person's sorrow becomes another's joy. One person's profit becomes another's loss. What a strange world. In the bank, too, just like in the circus, people play, big-time, but with other people's money—people they call clients, or savers, or investors, or, if you're me, stupid children.

As I grew older, I fell in love with Latin. I don't know how it happened. Maybe I'd actually fallen for my teacher, or else I was fascinated by the challenge of saving a "dead" language from oblivion. Even now I often use Latin proverbs because I love them so much. They give the impression that I'm a very cultured person—or perhaps that I'm just an old schoolmarm, who can say.

Later I dreamed of becoming a doctor. Certainly much better than the dream of becoming a nun, even though, either way, the goal remained the same: to save other people. A doctor's mission is to save bodies; a nun's is to save lost souls.

Come to think of it, there's another thing that doctors and nuns have in common: the color white. It's still my favorite color, along with yellow. Here I need to digress for a moment so I can talk about the blessed color white. I went to therapy for a long time, both individual and group. My ex-psychoanalyst, Simone, a very talented guy, had seen that this color was at the root of my deepest malaise. White is a symbol of purity among many different peoples. It gets dirty in a flash. That's the root of its fragility. A color that considers itself the absolute best can't abide sharing or competition. The worrisome thing is that white is the symbol of death, even though people immediately think of black, which they associate with mourning. In many cultures, however, Islamic culture for example, the dead man is placed in the grave wrapped in a white sheet.

"You're fragile because you tend toward the absolute," Simone told me once.

"I want to be a respectable person," I replied.

"Do you want to be a respectable person or a perfect person?"

"Why do I have to choose?"

"You want to be perfect."

"I don't know."

"You need to accept the other colors."

"I don't understand."

"Life is made up of compromises, Patrizia."

"I don't like compromises," I replied angrily.

"The world isn't just black or white."

"I want to be courageous."

I don't know why I gave that answer. "I want to be courageous." Even now, I sometimes happen to think of those words. Courage? What does it mean to *be courageous*? I think that the word "courage" represents the fundamental value of my personality. Being courageous means a great deal to me. It's an act of maturity. First of all, it means respecting myself and others. Being respectful of the world; looking at myself in the mirror and feeling no shame; having self-respect and being proud of myself and the things that I do. Having courage also means never losing sight of your own dignity and not being afraid to be judged. Living with your head held high, not hiding.

In political and spiritual terms, white is also the symbol of peace. This presents no problems. I'm against war and I want peace to spread throughout the world. Pictures of dead people, of terror attacks, of bombings, these upset me and make me feel bad, very bad. But can we rid the world of suffering? Can we get along without war? Is it possible for us all to live together in peace, in spite of our differences? This brings out the candy striper deep inside me.

Out of all these dreams and plans, in the end I chose to work at the bank. Someone might well ask: Why? To tell the truth, I don't really know. Maybe I wanted to be like my father, who worked for a bank. Oh, poor daddy, he died before his fortieth birthday. My mother, for her part, left me an orphan before she turned fifty. It's hard to be an only child and an orphan at the same time. I so wanted to have a sister or brother.

While it might be hard to understand the motivations behind my decision, I am able to tell the story of my initiation into the world of banking. As far as that goes, things are much clearer. At university I studied economics. I wanted to work and I wanted to be independent. I was convinced then, and I am still now, that work is the pathway to emancipation for women. There is no such thing as independence and freedom without work. I believe strongly in this sound and basic feminist principle. I thought that by studying economics I'd have more opportunity. And I was right. Many of my friends, both male and female, chose to study the humanities and their professional choices have been more limited than mine.

Right after taking my degree in economics, I started work on my master's degree and then I did a couple of internships at the bank. It was clear from the very beginning that I was cut out for the work. I had personality and ambition. I was ready to make a career for myself . . . *Career*. I hate that word more than any other in the world. Fucking career. Once I picked up the dictionary and ripped out the page where that word appeared. What a relief, how satisfying! But it's all temporary.

Unfortunately, ripping pages out of the dictionary isn't enough to eliminate odious words and concepts. Maybe we need to learn to coexist with them, to accept their presence. They're like shadows that are with us wherever we go. I don't know anyone who's been able to get rid of his or her own shadow. If you really think about it, your shadow is an extension of your body. It's just like your nose, your ears, your hand, or your foot.

* * *

The paths of life can be broken down into two kinds: uphill and downhill. The first kind are more challenging and treacherous. I remember a trip I took to San Francisco a few years ago. I've never seen streets like that. You get so scared seeing scooters, cars, buses, and especially the cable cars going straight up without flipping over, as if they were climbing a tree.

Flipping over while going uphill is a real disaster. And as we all know disasters come without warning and at top speed. At that point, all you can do is chase after them—even though it's often an exercise in futility, there's no alternative. What can you do? Try to slow them down as they careen, limit the damage. It takes an enormous effort to stop them, perhaps a minor miracle.

If I were a real fortune-teller, I'd be able to predict the future. Unfortunately I'm a fake fortune-teller trying to pass herself off as a gypsy, hoping she won't be unmasked. So far, it's worked out pretty darn well. Will it last? Let's hope so. The mission is a very delicate one.

This time, the greatest disaster since I started living as a gypsy is waiting for me at the camp, on an evening that seems just like any other. One look at Medina's face is all it takes to grasp the scope of the catastrophe. Her usual smile is lost in the midst of something indecipherable. Her words tremble in her mouth. She's very upset.

"Patrizia, something awful has happened."

"Don't call me Patrizia! My name is Drabarimos. Have they discovered our secret?" I reply, irritated.

"No."

"Then what's happened?"

"A girl from San Salvario was raped."

"Oh my God!"

"They're blaming us," she adds.

"What?!"

Medina doesn't care much for beating around the bush and comes straight to the point. A young girl from the neighborhood has accused the twins Drago and Jonathan of rape. As soon as the news got around, insults, intimidations, and provocations followed in short order. A number of Roma were attacked verbally and now everyone is afraid to go out. Our little camp, located next to Valentino Park, might be about to turn into a concentration camp, a prison without guards. Are we going to become the inmates and, at the same time, the jailers?

I go with Medina to the camp's little piazza, where a meeting is under way. Nearly everyone's there, and at the center of the crowd is Uncle Baros, the oldest of our group. I also see the twins, who are in tears. They're being interrogated to the sound of slaps and punches, but they deny everything categorically. They weren't in San Salvario all afternoon. They have ironclad alibis, too.

"We need someone who speaks Italian very well," says Uncle Baros, looking at me.

"Why, Uncle?" Medina asks.

"We need to explain to the *gadji* that we had nothing to do with it."

"You can count on me," I say.

The uncle thanks me and explains that the twins are innocent. If they'd done anything of the sort they would have run away immediately. They're a couple of bright boys and they know that there are certain things you absolutely cannot do. Rape is an unforgivable act. The repercussions will fall not only on the culprits, but on the entire community as well.

I decide to get moving. I call Luciano Terni. He's already aware of what's happened. I repeat to him what Uncle Baros said about the twins having nothing to do with it. He promises to help us. In the end we agree to meet tomorrow morning. "You'd better not leave the camp, I'll come to you," he advises me.

I met Luciano Terni during my first few weeks at the camp. I saw him arrive with a group of kids. Medina explained to me that Luciano does theater and is very fond of the Roma. I remember how our first meeting went very clearly.

"Drabarimos? I've never heard that name before," he told me with a handsome smile.

"It's not a name, it's a nickname."

"It has something to do with palm reading, doesn't it?"

"Exactly."

"And why do you use that name?"

"Apparently I have a gift for seeing the future."

"Usually fortune-tellers are old women, but you're quite young."

"Times change!"

He started laughing, and his laughter was so contagious I started laughing, too. Luciano is crazy about the theater. To him, everything is theater, performance. The world is a stage. To him, "Drabarimos," too, is a great theatrical performance: The gypsy woman is transformed into a fantastic actress capable of taking the whole production in hand, with grace and bravura, touching our hearts and giving us hope, the promise of happiness, dreams. We went back and forth a few more times, and then Luciano noticed a detail.

"Can I ask you something, Drabarimos?"

"Certainly."

"How come you speak such good Italian?"

"Because I'm from Turin."

"So you're a Piedmontese Sinti?"

"No. My folks were killed in a car crash right after we got here from Romania. I was very little. I grew up in an orphanage."

"I'm sorry to hear that."

"My greatest loss, aside from my parents, was that of my people's language."

I saw his face light up. Luciano smiled. He took my hand and kissed it. I didn't understand why he did it. All he said was: "Kissing a fortune-teller's hand brings luck." I don't know if that's true or if it was just a gallant thing to say. One sure thing is that his talents aren't limited to the theater. Luciano also has a way with women.

Over the past few months I've had the chance to get to know him better, and I must say I really like him. He's a cheerful, funny guy. For example, he has a truly remarkable gift for doing voices, especially politicians' voices. He makes us all laugh when he imitates Uncle Baros's voice. It's perfect; it sounds just like him. He really works hard to help the immigrants. He loves the Roma and he has a profound respect for them. I believe it's sincere.

In this night of fear and foreboding, I think constantly about the rape. I think about the young girl and her family. I also think about the twins, Drago and Jonathan. Were they telling the truth? I know that they're very good thieves, but to graduate from stealing to rape is no laughing matter. And after all, they came back to the camp instead of running away.

I can't get to sleep. When reality starts to look like a nightmare, it's best not to doze off, your sleep could easily become an extension of that nightmare. What's going to happen to us? How will this story end? Will the climb be merely laborious, or will it be catastrophic, will it end in a nasty rollover?

CHAPTER THREE
Roma rape a young Italian girl

S ince Tania got here, Aunt Quiz hasn't let us out of her sight. She might as well be marking man-to-man, as the soccer jargon would have it. She's doing an excellent job of espionage. But on whose behalf? No mystery there. For years now, my aunt has been working for my mother, who lives in Cosenza but wants to keep tabs on the delinquent son I've turned out to be. I'm constantly surveilled by two different women, Aunt Quiz and Natalia, the Ukrainian maid who comes to clean house every Wednesday. I don't even notice it anymore; in fact, I'm getting used to it. What can I do? When your fate is sealed, you might as well hoist the white flag. My privacy? That's certainly no priority in this blessed world, I might as well face facts.

This morning, too, Aunt Quiz is waiting for us at Giacomo's café, downstairs from our apartment building. It's an appointment that can't be missed. Tania is doing a great job of settling in. She doesn't mind my aunt's presence a bit. In fact, she likes her a lot: a little old lady full of energy and with such a positive attitude deserves nothing but admiration and respect, she says. The two of them are on a first-name basis and they exchange affectionate pecks on the cheek whenever they meet. They get along famously. I'm afraid they're plotting something behind my back, and that doesn't bode well for me. Tania is charmed: She's never seen an eighty-four-year-old spy go about her business with such devotion and precision. My lovely girlfriend chooses to turn a blind eye to these invasions of privacy. It's the same old story! Everyone has a right to live in peace without having to deal with spies, informants, moles, and other pains in the ass—and yet nobody seems to give a damn about poor Enzo Laganà's privacy.

The atmosphere in the café this morning is by no means cheerful. I see worried looks on everyone's faces. It's easy to guess the reason. The subject of the day goes without saying, not just here, but in every café in Italy. Soccer and politics can wait. The crime blotter takes absolute priority. Giacomo, the proprietor, seems chipper this morning, in spite of the grim circumstances. He's like the conductor of an orchestra. He skillfully supervises the statements of the various customers. Everyone wants the chance to pipe in. It's like a group therapy session. Bellezza's presence is missed.

"I blame the left and their open-door policy toward everyone," says a customer I've never seen before.

"Why do you always blame politics?" Giacomo retorts.

"The rape of a girl who could have been our daughter or granddaughter is a tragedy and that's it," comments a man in his seventies whose name I can never remember. He's a tailor with a shop on Via Silvio Pellico and he's still in business. These days, artisans like him are an endangered species in San Salvario.

"We have to make sure that these kinds of rapes never happen again," adds Giacomo in a constructive spirit.

Unfortunately the discussion veers off in another direction. Good old Giacomo loses control of the situation. A competition starts up to see who can make the most outrageous statement. A lady who works at the post office on Via Principe Tommaso declares that there's nothing to be done with the gypsies. They've always been a lost cause. All this talk of integration is a waste of time and an insult to our intelligence. After all, they've had centuries to adapt to our civilization, to our laws, to the rules of our civil society, but they've always done as they pleased. They've never once stopped making trouble and feeding our worst fears. They'll steal anything, including children. Sadly, we're going to have to face up to the fact that this gypsy race isn't, in fact, part of the human race. And then what should we do? Simple: proceed to sterilize their women without further delay. A gentleman I've never seen before picks up right where the woman leaves off and reminds all those present that there was someone (a guy with real balls) who'd already found a way to uproot this inferior race more than sixty years ago. The Nazi drift that the debate is starting to take persuades me to shut my ears. I'm happy that Aunt Quiz and Tania are staying out of this shitstorm. They're deep in a lengthy chat about how cold the Nordic countries are. My aunt has a horror of the cold. She always wonders how people are able to live in places where every winter it gets down to 15 degrees, or even to zero, and stays there. Usually when we talk about hell the first thing we think of is heat and flames, but it would be more appropriate to imagine hell covered in ice. Do humans have an easier time tolerating the heat or the cold? My aunt's question results in a nice vigorous debate.

I take advantage of the opportunity to glance at the newspaper, my own paper. The front-page headline doesn't leave a lot of room for interpretation. ROMA RAPE A YOUNG ITALIAN GIRL: You can't get clearer or more straightforward than that. This doesn't bode well. If it's true that you can tell a good day from the morning, then you can tell the tone of an article from its headline. Under which is yours truly's first and last name. Nice work, Enzo. I proceed to peruse my article, or rather the article that Salvini and Maritani have altered, manipulated, and falsified. A quick skim justifies my initial misgivings. They've added stuff, phrases and words I would never say, things like, "Turin is in a state of shock," "The situation could get out of hand," "People in Turin are getting angrier by the minute; it's impossible to say what might happen," and so on and so forth. What else should I have expected? To tell the truth, it could have gone even worse. They could have, for example, published a fabricated interview with the young girl who was raped, or slapped her picture on the front page. In the absence of clear facts and figures, the impulse is to improvise, make do, paper over the gaps, pander to the basest curiosities. This is our fucked-up profession.

Just to make sure I don't miss a thing, I go back to the front page, a touch masochistically. What am I trying to do? Ruin my day? Spoil my mood? I look to the left and see Salvini's editorial. Inevitable, whenever there's big news. This time he's chosen a combative headline: WHEN WILL WE FIGHT BACK?

A healthy, vigorious society is always possessed of antibodies to defend itself and, most importantly, to fight off infections. Italy is under anesthesia. That's the grim and inconvenient truth. At this point, we're an aged, weary nation. Why are we incapable of fighting back? This question demands an answer now more than ever in the face of the great tragedy that befell the city of Turin yesterday. In a working-class neighborhood, a fifteen-year-old girl was raped by two Roma. Something that beggars description. A respectable family destroyed by pain. [. . .] We need to raise our voices and shout: We are afraid. Yes, these violent foreigners are making our day-to-day lives unsafe. Everyone agrees that things can't go on like this. We need to have the courage and intellectual honesty to admit that there is a gypsy emergency in this blessed country. When will we fight back? When?

I fold up the paper and finish my cappuccino. I'm pretending to listen to Aunt Quiz and Tania when I see Luciano Terni come in. In one hand he's holding a copy of the newspaper that I just leafed through. He waves it with an indecipherable smile.

He's a stage actor, he can speak with his body. He even goes so far as to completely ignore Tania's lovely presence. He's usually a gentleman, unfailingly attentive to the little things, matters of form. Because, as people say, form and content are really the same thing. I've heard this interesting saying a great many times. I have to confess that I've never fully understood it.

He starts off with, "Congratulations on the front-page story," just to mock me.

"Don't be an asshole."

"I'm being serious. Wait and see, you'll finally take home some major journalism award."

"Come on, cut it out."

"At this point there's no end to the stupidity, vulgarity, and offensiveness," he adds.

"Let's go outside, I want a cigarette."

Luciano is an easygoing guy, but when he loses his temper he turns into a monster and I'm not interested in being one of his victims. I take him outside to forestall any unpleasant surprises. I don't want any two-bit tantrums, especially not in front of Tania. There's nothing better than a cigarette to soothe a troubled soul. I light up a filter-tip MS, alias Mortal Smokes. I offer him one as well, but he turns it down with a less-than-diplomatic gesture. That's never happened before. The situation is serious. Did he come to pick a fight? But why?

"Do you want to explain this headline to me?" he jumps in angrily.

"It's a disgrace."

"But the article has your byline."

"I didn't choose the headline. That's the copy editors, the news editors, the managing editors. You know that perfectly well."

"And what about what's in the article?"

"Those aren't all my words," I point out.

"I can't believe you'd just wash your hands of it like that."

"But it's the truth," I insist.

Luciano can't let go of the headline in particular: ROMA RAPE A YOUNG ITALIAN GIRL. A masterpiece. A journalistic paragon that will be imitated. In his opinion, there's enough evidence to call this inciting a hate crime. What worries him is not so much the judicial side of things (no one cares about the Roma anyway), but the moral side. What the hell happened to the journalistic code of ethics? Is it right to criminalize the entire Roma people? It never occurs to anyone to include a rapist's birthplace in a headline: Turinese, Roman, American, French, Brazilian, German, Japanese, British, etc. But when it comes to the Roma in particular and immigrants in general, it's a free-for-all. People are never held responsible for their positions and statements. Libel is a crime that applies only to certain segments of society.

Little by little, Luciano calms down. I tell him how things went. I dwell in particular on the fact that Salvini ditched my conditional in favor of the present indicative. Normally, I don't explain my work to anyone. But I really value Luciano's friendship. After clearing things up, we go back into the café and I offer to treat him to an espresso. He accepts. A good sign of reconciliation. He apologizes to Tania for not saying hello earlier. Of course he tries to mend fences with Aunt Quiz, too, who appreciates the gesture. Luckily, Luciano has an extraordinary ability to spread cheer. All he needs are a couple of wisecracks, jokes, or imitations.

* * *

I go to the Madama Cristina market to do some grocery shopping. I'm planning to make a nice fish-and-vegetable lunch. Something good and easy that won't take me too long to make. As I'm chatting with the man at the seafood stall, I hear someone shouting. I turn around and see that Mario Bellezza has lost it; he's shouting at two Roma women with two small children.

"Get the fuck out of the way! Nobody wants you people around! Gang of rapists!"

"What on earth are you talking about? Stop making a scene," snaps one of the two women; she's dressed in yellow.

"The rapists come from your camp," Bellezza insists.

"Stop talking nonsense. We didn't have anything to do with it."

"You'll pay for this," he goes on, his tone aggressive.

"If you keep threatening us, I'll report you to the police," the woman adds.

One of the children starts crying. The woman in yellow hugs the child and tries to comfort him. One detail catches my attention: This is first time I've heard a Rom speak such perfect Italian, right down to the correct use of the formal. I'm curious to know where she studied the language. This might be a chance to dig a little deeper and write a nice positive piece about immigration and integration (though that last word is a real pain in the ass). An immigrant woman—and what's more a Rom—who has so completely mastered the Italian language deserves to be on the front page of a major daily, to be invited to appear on TV. Unfortunately, the mass media is only interested in trash. We need a vast media revolution to put things right.

Bellezza notices my presence. He strides over with a confident gait, despite the weight of his beer belly. The heavy panting is by now just a normal part of his breathing, a sort of trademark. To say nothing of the sweat. The stench reaches you even from a distance.

"My dear Enzo, it's time to make a clean sweep. Let's get the gypsies off our fucking backs."

"You scared the children," I point out.

"What children are you talking about! These are nothing but little monsters, future rapists."

"Come on!"

"I'm not kidding. We need to castrate them immediately," he says, piling on.

"Stop exaggerating."

"By the way, I'd like to thank you for your article in today's paper. Congratulations on the wonderful headline."

Now I have no more doubts. It's the umpteenth piece of proof that the headline is a disgrace, a real piece of shit. Anything that Bellezza likes must automatically be a disgrace. My reasoning is impeccable: Bellezza's vision of the world is the opposite of mine. We only have one thing in common: We're both southern Italians. We're dirty Southerners. But while Bellezza does everything he can to forget that fact, yours truly proudly and publicly lays claim to it: I'm a second-generation dirty Southerner. Aren't you impressed?

"Enzo, are we going to see you tonight at the demonstration?"

"What demonstration?"

"The one in San Salvario."

"Do you mean the torchlight march?" I ask, trying to clear up the confusion.

Now, there's quite a difference between a demonstration and a torchlight march. It's always a good idea to call things by their proper names. Otherwise, words will lose their meanings and no one will be able to understand a thing. Bellezza puts everything into political terms: those who agree with him and those who don't. In other words, he divides the world in two: good and evil, good guys and bad guys, the just and the unjust, black and white, and so on and so forth. The moral of the story is always the same: You need to take sides, no ifs, ands, or buts. Always. What does all this have to with politics? As far as I know, politics—at least in the best sense of the word—is the art of mediation, the ability to resolve conflicts peacefully. I have a well-founded suspicion. When Bellezza talks about politics, he actually means something else: war. I don't think it's possible to convince him otherwise or to have a cool and considered argument with him. It strikes me as a waste of time.

"By the way, have you read the letter that the Virgin of Via Ormea wrote?"

"Who? What Virgin of Via Ormea?!"

"Virginia, the young girl who was raped."

"So that's what she's calling herself now?"

"Yes, even though she deserves to be called Saint," he insists.

"Though first she'd have to be beatified."

"Saint immediately!"

"There are no such things as living saints."

"There's an exception to every rule," he retorts.

"So what did she write?"

Bellezza catches me up on the latest developments. Virginia, alias the Virgin of Via Ormea, has written a brief open letter to the public. Bellezza recites the finale for me; he's learned it by heart: "As a Catholic, I can only forgive those who hurt me. I forgive you. I forgive you. I forgive you." No one has ever seen a young girl so pure of heart and soul. So mature. Even in the face of the harsh ordeal that she's lived through, she rejects hatred and vengeance. Bellezza plunges into a lengthy and heartfelt speech of praise. I have to admit that he's better informed than the wire services. He has all the credentials necessary to rival Reuters. The young girl has received messages of support and solidarity from around the world. There is even talk of an invitation to the Vatican for an audience with the Holy Father and of another to meet with the President of the Republic. Everyone's talking about the Virgin of Via Ormea, and now they'll be talking about San Salvario, too. There's no doubt about it. The mass media, especially the television networks, don't miss a trick; they've offered her a handsome fee for a brief appearance or a short exclusive interview. But her answer was no. At least for now.

This whole thing about the rape is starting to stress me out. Luckily, Tania and I are leaving tomorrow to spend a week in the mountains. I need a break. When I get back the whole thing will be over and no one will even remember it. Unfortunately, the trauma will persist, both for the person subjected to the rape and for her family. My cell phone rings. The call's provenance is unmistakable.

"Enzu', when are you coming home?"

"I'm out buying groceries."

"How long will it take you?"

"Why are you asking me these questions?"

"Lunch is ready. We're just about to sit down."

"What lunch!? I don't understand, Mamma."

"I'm at home with your aunt Giovanna and with Tania."

"At home? In San Salvario?"

"Yes."

"When did you get to Turin?"

"About an hour ago."

"Why didn't you tell me you were coming today?"

A stupid question. Who would think of asking the financial police to call ahead and let you know they'll be doing an inspection? Of course the point was to surprise me. My mother's an expert, and one of these days she'll give me a heart attack. It's just a matter of time. Did she know that Tania was there? Why, of course she knew. She'd been informed the minute Tania had arrived. Now I'm in a world of shit. Where will she sleep? In the living room? Should I check into a hotel with Tania? What a mess! I have to keep my cool. It's just a matter of spending tonight in the same apartment. Tomorrow Tania and I are leaving for the mountains. My mother's a master at playing these games.

I hurry home. The atmosphere there is quite cheerful. This

is the first time my mother and Tania have met. Now I understand the real reason for her unannounced visit. She wanted to meet Tania in person. The reports from her two spies weren't enough anymore. It's all calculated, then. Of course, I shouldn't overlook the crucial role played by Aunt Quiz. I don't know how my mother managed to make lunch so quickly. She probably brought everything ready-made from Cosenza.

"Have you seen what a nice surprise we pulled off?" Tania asks me with a smile.

"So you knew about it?"

"Of course I did. We had a long talk on the phone yesterday."

"Why didn't you say anything?"

"Then it wouldn't have been a surprise."

"Right."

We sit down at the table. I'm not all that hungry. I pick at my food to avoid drawing attention to myself. Tania's attitude surprises me. She's quite relaxed; in fact, she's enjoying herself. She's smiling ear to ear. Impossible to imagine a more harmonious scene. Women blessedly content among women. I feel like dead weight.

After the coffee I decide to get out of their hair. I leave Tania in good hands and head over to the newspaper.

* * *

I get there shortly before the beginning of the torchlight march, around 6:30 P.M. The marchers decide to kick off the event in Via Ormea, right below the young girl's apartment. A gesture of solidarity with the family. I see prominent political figures from the left, the center, and the right. An exceedingly rare example of political harmony. Lots of people compliment me on the article in this morning's paper; they specifically praise that goddamn headline. I accept their thanks with great restraint. I came expecting a subdued torchlight march, with plenty of candles and rainbow banners; instead I see lots of signs with unsettling messages: "We're Through with Gypsies"; "Down with Bleeding-Heart Liberals"; "Get the Rapists Away from Our Little Girls"; "Gypsies Are Rapists"; "No More Sex Fiends in Our Cities."

At the head of the procession are Virginia's cousin Giuliano, Mario Bellezza, and every last member of his committee. I meet a friend who's a Juventus supporter. He travels in circles also frequented by soccer hooligans. He tells me something strange is happening: A group of hooligans is planning to teach the Roma a lesson, but that's all he knows. I ask him about the route of the torchlight march and he tells me that it was organized by them, by the hooligans. This is the first time I've ever heard of soccer hooligans organizing torchlight marches. Quite the qualitative leap. It's also a real scoop, a story about violent soccer fanatics converting to pacifism. How could such a thing have taken place and gone completely unnoticed? A genuine miracle.

Before the march gets going, Cousin Giuliano reads the letter from the Virgin of Via Ormea out loud.

Life is a beautiful, divine gift. We are born, we live, and we die. It's like an extraordinary journey during which many things happen to us, some good, others less good. Jesus taught us to accept evil and cruelty without hatred, resentment, and a desire for revenge. At this difficult moment in my journey through this beautiful world, I'd like to keep in mind the example set by Our Jesus. Sorrow and grief should never make us forget our humanity and our goodness. We must remain good. We mustn't let ourselves be led astray from our Christian and human values.

I'd like to thank all of you who are giving me your support, first of all my beloved family, my friends, and the residents of San Salvario and of Turin. I love you all so much.

Last of all, as a Catholic, I can only forgive those who hurt me. I forgive you. I forgive you. I forgive you.

The letter tugs at the heartstrings. Some people can't choke back their tears, especially during the last part where she repeats, "I forgive you." Her cousin stops reading to dry his tears. The crowd reacts. All this translates into a stream of anti-Roma insults. A long soccer-stadium chorus of jeers.

I walk with the demonstrators like a sheep with its flock. We cover the length of Via Ormea, then turn right when we come to Corso Vittorio Emanuele II. I don't understand why the procession is turning right instead of left. Usually torchlight marches head for the center of town, where powerful instutions are concentrated. When we cross the Umberto I bridge, my doubts start to grow. At the corner of Corso Moncalieri, the procession turns right again. At that point I realize that we're going straight to the little Roma camp next to Valentino Park. And indeed, a short while later, we stop right outside it. No trace of the Roma. Where have they gone? Maybe they got out in time. What a relief.

The hooligans' party doesn't take long to get started. Openly violent and racist chants directed not only against the Roma, but against immigrants as a whole. I even hear people insulting Neapolitans and southern Italians more generally. Some members of the citizens' associations try to cool tempers, but it's all pointless.

Two hooligans break off from the procession and enter a trailer. The shouts of the crowd grow louder, and I can't tell if it's to further incite them or try to make them see reason. Such confusion. A few seconds later the trailer goes up in flames and then it's another trailer's turn. A Roma woman dressed in yellow (the same one I saw this morning at the market) goes over to one of the trailers in flames.

"Wait, I'm begging you. There's a little boy inside," she shouts in desperation.

"Gypsies in the ovens! Gypsies in the ovens!" a group of masked young men chants in unison.

"Murderers!" the woman shouts.

"Gypsies in the ovens!"

Other trailers catch fire. The woman in yellow, defying the flames, lunges into the trailer before the crowd's astonished eyes. After a seemingly endless moment, we see her emerge with a child in her arms. Only a mother would do such a thing to save her child. She takes a few steps and then collapses to the ground, unconscious. A number of demonstrators rush to her aid. In the midst of the general chaos Turin's most notorious animal rights activist, Irene Morbidi, appears out of thin air, shouting: "Let's save the little doggies. They may have been left behind in the trailers." We immediately hear sirens. Then they're all there at once: police, Carabinieri, firefighters, ambulances. I've never understood why they always show up together, and always late.

* * *

I walk into the newsroom on Via Garibaldi. No sooner do I turn on my computer than I see Maritani coming. He's waving a sheet of paper. This is a wire service report that just came in:

> Turin, 8:25 P.M. Two Roma, a woman and a boy, were taken to Molinette Hospital in serious condition. The camp they were living in, near Valentino Park, was set ablaze. It should be remembered that a number of Turin's citizens organized a torchlight march for this afternoon to protest a rape that took place yesterday in the San Salvario neighborhood. A young Italian girl, now known as the Virgin of Via Ormea, was raped by twin Roma brothers who live in the camp that was burned.

After reading the wire report, Maritani starts in with the commentary. He loves adding his two cents because it demonstrates his ability to read not only between, but also above, below, behind, and in front of the lines. Personally, I don't care much for this little game. Which is why I fucking interrupt him in a hurry.

"These weren't overemotional demonstrators, Angelo."

"What are you talking about?"

"I was there and I saw it all. Everything had been planned out, every last detail."

"Who were they, Enzo?"

"Thugs, a gang of fascist bastards."

"Come with me to my office."

"I'd like to write up an eyewitness account first."

"You can do that later. Right now we need to call the editor in chief."

"Can't that wait?"

No! Maritani updates me on our editor in chief. For the first time in a long time, he's been invited back on TV—on *Rear Window*, Italy's highest-rated talk show. At this very moment he's in the studio for the live broadcast. It goes without saying that the topic of tonight's show is the rape of the young girl in Turin.

Luckily the conference call on speakerphone with Salvini doesn't last long. There's no need to stretch the broth. He wants the latest news. I briefly tell him exactly what happened. I concentrate on the torchlight march, or rather the exercise in vigilante justice. He says nothing. Maybe he's in a hurry. In any case, he limits himself to expressing his appreciation for our great show of professional ethics. I choose not to retort. What good would it do? It might be useful to discuss the newspaper's blessed editorial approach and offer some criticism (constructive, of course) concerning the regrettable choice of headlines. Maritani listens passively, breaking in only to confirm, using words and phrases like: sure, certainly, of course, obviously, that's logical, logically, right, right, of course, exactly, precisely, perfect, perfectly, and so on. He always uses the same words when he speaks with Salvini. Not so much as a crumb of creativity.

In the end we tell our editor in chief to break a leg; he'll be on live TV in just a few minutes. These appearances are not only helpful to him, but to the newspaper as well. Maritani is very careful to make this point. He invites me to stay and watch the talk show with him. I diplomatically decline the invitation. I'm pretty sure I won't miss anything important. All I'll need to do is read Salvini's editorial tomorrow morning. Salvini has a unique talent: He can repeat the same ideas in the same words over and over again. Everyone knows his slogan: Repeating yourself is an act of intellectual consistency.

I say goodbye to Maritani and go to my office to write my piece on the torchlight march. I can't get the picture of the trailers on fire out of my mind. I can tell that this grim story won't end soon. The flames won't be easily quenched.

At this point it's probably wise to stay in Turin. I'll have to ask Tania if we can put off our departure until tomorrow. There's no other solution, the situation is spinning out of control. This is not the ideal moment to go hiking in the mountains of Piedmont. Vacations demand equanimity and peace of mind. And right now, we're in the middle of an emergency.

People often say that if you haven't got your health, you haven't got anything. And it's true. When work becomes a sickness, then the best thing to do is sacrifice it without a second thought. To hell with it all—work, money, career, success. For me, working at the bank was not only a disease; it was a curse, a true cross to bear. Something that didn't end when office hours were over. I carried it with me everywhere. It was like a newborn baby who couldn't tear himself away from his mother's breast for even a second. Relaxation was a luxury I couldn't afford. Then suddenly something happened. I started to look reality right in the face. I couldn't keep running away from myself all the time. I realized I was addicted, that's right, addicted to my work. I worked more and more, day and night, at home on the weekends, even during the few days I was forced to take off at Christmas. I can safely say that I was living the life of a robot, a machine programmed to perform a few given tasks, with no will of its own.

Since a robot can only possess a professional life, there's no point in discussing its private life. Nothing much to speak of, I had very little room to maneuver. A private life was not a priority. For that reason, my love life doesn't exactly abound with details; just three major romances, three names: Giancarlo, Salvo, and Mauro.

I met Giancarlo in high school. I discovered sex and cigarettes with him; I only found out about joints a few years later. To everything there is a season. It was a romance full of innocence.

At that age we truly are outside of reality. We live in the clouds, not on planet Earth. We believe that love is eternal, and so we're inflexible. Of course the disappointment and the frustration are enormous, they're genuine tragedies. When a relationship reaches the end of the line, we feel as if the world is falling down around us. The thing I especially remember about Giancarlo is how sweet he was. He was a sensitive boy. He never let me cry alone. He'd cry with me, he never got embarrassed. A very rare quality in this world so full of men who pretend to be strong, but who, deep down, conceal great fragilities.

At university I fell in love with Salvo. We traveled together a lot. We saw all of Italy aboard his beautiful Yamaha. We explored the world, from Europe and Asia to Africa and America. He was a fantastic travel partner, a true adventurer, but he couldn't be my life partner. Why not? Salvo wasn't the faithful type. He had no control over his own sexual impulses. I found that unacceptable. On this point I feel exactly as most women do: To love means first and foremost to be faithful. In any case, our breakup was amicable. I heard from mutual friends that he moved to Germany for work. Neither one of us tried to track the other down. And that's fine. *Omnia fert aetas*, time bears away all things.

My last great romance was with Mauro. A first-rate lawyer. We even got married. So actually I'm a divorcée. In short, I didn't miss a thing. We were husband and wife for almost three years. Then everything fell apart. He worked all the time and so did I. We were always stressed out. We didn't talk much. After a certain point, we felt like strangers. The breakup was painless. We each went our own way. Afterwards, though, he was luckier than me. A couple years later, he met a nursery school teacher. They got married, had two children, and now they're living happily ever after, or so it would seem from the outside looking in.

Probably Mauro was looking for a woman who could care for him as if he were a child. And what's wrong with that? Most men are looking to replace their mothers with a woman whose name they can change, a woman they can call "wife." I, on the other hand, have never found anyone who really interested me, maybe because I never seriously searched. Seek and ye shall find. Or perhaps I simply never had a clear idea of what it was I wanted. Life is like that: When we want to make it more complicated it's only too happy to help out, it's eager to make the job easier for us. Simplifying is an art, a difficult skill to master.

As for the delicate question of whether to have children—or, let me immediately correct myself: whether to have a child (let's take one thing at a time)—of course I've given the idea a thought, once or twice. No mentally sound woman can pretend to ignore it entirely. Nature doesn't kid around. Of course you can evade the question, but all evasions hit a wall, come to an end. There've been times in my life when I thought about my blessed biological clock with a certain insistence, when I was married, for instance. I have to admit that Mauro was in favor of it, especially at the beginning, but then we got caught up in a discussion about priorities. Having a child was important to us, but not super important. We had other priorities. That damn couple, for example: Mr. Job and Mrs. Career.

After Mauro, I had brief affairs. Minor amusements, passing flings. I often found myself playing the role of the mistress, and, I have to say, I had my fun. Being involved with a married man is more exciting because of the suspense. Unfaithful husbands are afraid, and I found their fear very amusing. I was very curious to learn all about the various strategies of betrayal. Each guy had his own plan. But you can't just have a good plan; you also have to know how to put it into practice. That's why being a skillful liar is so fundamental. All it takes is a tiny mistake and everything goes to pieces. In some cases, the consequences are serious. The price you pay is very high.

* * *

Late in the morning, Luciano shows up while we're talking with Uncle Baros about what to do. The situation is serious and there's a real chance things will spin out of control. Luciano did his best to reassure us, but in vain. We're all afraid, especially the twins and their family. We don't know what's going to happen. Uncle Baros believes that the best solution is to leave this place in a hurry. Luciano doesn't agree. We listen silently as the two of them talk it out.

"To leave now means running away."

"What else can we do?" asks the uncle, throwing his arms in the air.

"If you go away now, everyone's going to believe that you're guilty of or at the very least complicit in the rape," Luciano warns.

"We're innocent."

"I'm sure of that, Uncle."

"We need to protect our women and children," Uncle Baros insists.

"We need to find a solution," says Luciano.

"You're our friend. Give us your advice."

"You should go to the police."

"Why should we turn ourselves in? We haven't done anything wrong."

Luciano explains to us with great patience that going to the police doesn't mean turning in the twins, just clarifying our position. While running away, at this point, could be viewed as an admission of guilt. I think it's a reasonable argument. You can't always run away. When someone is innocent, he has the right, the duty, to shout his innocence from the rooftops. To fight to the bitter end for the sake of the truth. In these cases, fear is no help; in fact, it's actually harmful. What's needed is courage. That's my secret weapon. So I decide to speak up, to bolster Luciano's position.

"I understand Uncle Baros's fears. But we need to stay here," I say, my voice charged with determination.

"We don't have anyplace to go, and we're afraid," Medina adds.

"You shouldn't be afraid. You aren't alone. I'll go in to the police station with you, if you like," Luciano suggests.

Uncle Baros trusts him. They decide to go to the police with the twins. I think it's the right solution. Luciano's presence gives us a great deal of confidence. And that's something we really need. The real danger at this point is being isolated. Luciano takes me aside; he wants to tell me something important.

"You need to be very careful."

"It's true, the situation is terribly tense," I reply.

"There's a wave of collective hysteria."

"Can I come with you to the police station?" I ask.

"Better not."

"Why?"

"You don't have ID. Why run the risk?"

"Are you afraid they'll send me away?"

"You never know," he answers with a smile.

I often forget that I'm living without papers. In other words, I'm an illegal. I told the people at the camp that I had a residential visa, but that unfortunately I had been unable to renew it. And so I was transformed from a legal immigrant into an illegal one. A very credible story. Luciano explained to me that this is a fairly common problem among immigrants in Italy. It's like blackmail. Visa renewal is extremely complicated; for instance, they demand a regularly registered employment contract, and it has to be open-ended.

Luciano leaves with Uncle Baros and the twins. This is the worst things have been since I first set foot in this camp. To ease the tension I decide to swing by the Madama Cristina market anyway. I can't stand being cooped up here like a prisoner. I'm suffocating. I want to stretch my legs. As I'm leaving, Medina calls to me.

"Where are you going, Drabarimos?"

"I'm going to the market. Do you need anything?"

"Let's go together."

"That's not a good idea, Medina."

"How long are we going to have to stay shut up in this place?" she asks me, a hint of anger in her voice.

"Let's hope not for long."

In the end, I go to the market with her. We carry Demir and Zafira with us. At this point, I'm getting used to the children. When they call me "mama"—I feel something stir inside me.

I tell myself that this is like a thunderstorm. It'll pass, of course it will, only we don't know how much damage it will do. After all, we're talking about the rape of a young girl. The question that obsesses me is this: Who told the truth, the twins, Drago and Jonathan, or the girl from San Salvario? Someone is certainly lying.

When we get to the market, I immediately sense the atmosphere. We're getting angry looks. I do my best not to be intimidated by them. I take a quick stroll around to buy some fruits and vegetables. The air seems almost too heavy to breathe. I'm looking a fruit stall over when I hear a very loud voice behind me. I whip around and find myself face-to-face with that damn Bellezza. What a name—it means "beauty"! If you spend any time in San Salvario, especially at the market, it's practically impossible not to know him. He's an ugly man, nasty and vulgar. Every time I see him in the distance, I head the other way. I don't like talking to him or listening to what he has to say. Medina is tremendously afraid of Bellezza. She can't get a word out in his presence. I don't care either way about him.

"What are you doing here?" he asks, his tone challenging.

"Shopping for groceries," I reply, keeping my cool.

"Don't make me laugh."

"As you can see, I'm making purchases," I add.

"You people are always looking for trouble."

"We're respectable people."

"You're a bunch of rapists."

After this little back-and-forth I decide it's time to leave. Little Demir has taken fright and he's started crying. It's definitely not a good idea to give the man an opportunity to humiliate us in the middle of the market. He likes these kinds of situations because he treats them like political rallies, platforms from which to trumpet his propaganda. Luciano told me that Bellezza is the founder of a right-wing organization aimed at pitting the people of San Salvario against immigrants, us Roma in particular.

I have a sneaking feeling that things aren't going to stop here. This verbal violence is nothing but a prelude to physical violence. I'm catching a whiff of something truly ugly. I'm starting to worry about walking down the street alone. I'd better head straight back to the camp. I prefer to stay there, with the others, in the hope that the thunderstorm will soon pass.

In any case, this isn't the first time I've had an unpleasant encounter with Bellezza, or maybe I should call him Bruttezza—ugliness. One time, maybe five or six months ago, I can't remember exactly, I was with Medina and the two little ones. We were close to the Madama Cristina market when a woman in her early fifties started berating us for no good reason.

"Get the hell out of here!" she shouted.

"Where is it that you think we should go, Signora?" I asked her patiently.

"Just go back where you came from."

"Italy is where we came from. It's our country."

"Italy isn't your country and it never will be. Never!"

"You're wrong there, Signora."

"You're all just thieves."

"No, we're perfectly respectable people."

"Don't make me laugh," she snapped sarcastically.

At that point I went over to her and explained that we're Piedmontese Sinti. Our ancestors came to the Piedmont region in the Middle Ages. That means Italy has been our homeland for centuries. We didn't just get here. The lady was flabbergasted and had nothing to say. A group of curious lookers-on had gathered; they'd caught a whiff of a fight. Far be it from me to insult anyone else. But I'm not about to be insulted for no good reason. That lady definitely asked for it. So I decided to go on the offensive, arming myself with, among other weapons, irony. I took advantage of one very important detail.

"You aren't from Turin originally, are you, Signora?" I asked.

"What kind of a question is that?"

"Just answer."

"I've lived in Turin since I was five."

"Ah . . . now I understand your accent. Where were you born?"

"In Sicily."

"Oh, so you're a dirty Southerner," I say to her, my tone playful.

Just like that, bull's eye. Now you do the math for yourself, people. Let's see who the real outsider is. And, most importantly, just who needs to go back where they came from. The lady is embarrassed. She wants to run away but she can't. There's no way out except to apologize, and she won't do that. All right. A public humiliation in the middle of the market will have to do. She slips away without a sound. The crowd enjoyed the show they'd just seen: *The Dirty Southerner and the Two Gypsy Women*. As for me, I was quite pleased with the outcome. Maybe we'd be able to enjoy a little peace and quiet in that market from then on.

I hate arrogance in all its forms, especially rudeness. It's time we stopped saying that the Roma are all thieves. The real thieves are elsewhere. Who does more harm: the Rom who steals a wallet or the bank that cheats its savers? Medina's husband is in prison for burglary. I have to wonder whether there are any bankers in prison. Who ever said that the law's the same for everyone?

My vacation in the mountains with Tania has been postponed because of yours truly's professional obligations. My physical presence is required in San Salvario. Unfortunately, they can't do without me. My mother has decided to go stay with Aunt Quiz. A sensible decision. An acceptable compromise. I can't quite see her in the same apartment with me and Tania. Everyone needs a little personal space. She's explained that she'll leave us alone, but only at night. That means that during the day she'll come and do whatever she pleases. This morning she showed up early and made a big spread for breakfast, with plenty of Calabrian pastries. She's treating us like a couple of newlyweds.

In fact, as far as that's concerned, her chief objective is to hustle me to the altar as soon as is humanly possible. Will she succeed? Well, only time will tell. In the meantime she leaves no stone unturned and never stops pressuring me. Last time she told me: "*Figliu mia, tieni quarantun anni. Te manca 'n annu pe' te spusa'. Dopu 'un se po' fa' chiù nente.*" ("My son, you're forty-one. You have just one more year to get married. After that, there's nothing to be done.") My mother is convinced of one thing: Once a man crosses the fatal threshold that is his forty-second birthday, chances are he'll stay a bachelor forever. There's no point trying to convince her otherwise. She thinks I'm not happy the way I am. I'll only be happy, truly happy, with my better half at my side, a lovely *mogliera*. You try and explain to her that being a bachelor—to be clear, an eligible bachelor like myself—is the very height of happiness. When it comes to holy matrimony, I have to admit that our opinions on the subject are wildly divergent. Ah well; you can't agree on everything. The important thing, from my own very modest point of view, is not to bust other people's balls. That's the fundamental principle underlying all civil society. In fact, what do extremists do? They force other people to follow *their* path to salvation, the absolute truth, whether they like it or not. Especially if they don't. And it's for this very reason that extremists are a real fucking pain in my ass.

The breakfast made by my mother, aka Mrs. I Do, doesn't pass without comment. Tania is quite impressed. Of course, she doesn't pass up the chance to needle me a little.

"You're as spoiled as a little prince."

"Let's not go overboard."

"I've never seen a mother like yours."

"Where I come from I'm hardly an unusual case."

"God bless the Mediterranean *mamma*."

"They're not all sunshine and flowers."

"Why are you complaining?"

"I'm not complaining. I'm just trying to tell you that being the son has its downsides."

"Downsides?! You call a wonderful breakfast like this a downside?"

"Let me try and explain."

I launch into an extended comparison of the Mediterranean mother with her Nordic counterpart. Then I talk about the life of a mama's boy, which has its pluses and minuses. I base my argument on a case that I know all too well: that of Enzo Laganà. Still, I take care not to slip into the realm of the personal. It's much wiser to stick to generic observations. Now then, being the center of attention isn't always a good thing. The danger is that you continue to feel like a child and act like one too. A little pampering is great, but too much pampering is bad, very bad. I understand Tania's astonishment: She sees the world through the eyes of a northerner. The Mediterranean mama's boy is an undeniable fact. But it would be unfair to put all the blame on him. Can we talk about society? Isn't it in the business of over-mothering? What about the state? The government? The parliament? Labor unions? Schools? The church? Over-mothering is everywhere. Italy is a country that is proud to over-mother.

Tania doesn't listen to me with anything like the proper amount of attention. I realize that I'm talking bullshit. She's bored, there's no mistaking the fact. In part because it's not the first, the second, or even the third time that she's heard about the Mediterranean mama's boy. At this point, she's listened to this record so many times it turns her stomach. Now I'd like to change the subject, but I need to do it with great diplomacy. I don't want to seem like I've been beaten, like I'm a man without convictions, ideas, views. There's a word that I like: views. Always in the plural. One view, singular, isn't good for anything; it's like a single swallow in springtime. Having views means that you're someone with a system of thought, a vision of the world. And this is a fine concept that truly impresses everyone: a handsome vision of the world, solid and internally coherent. Unfortunately I can't seem to change the damn subject. It's a little like quicksand: the further in you go, the more you complicate your own existence. Retracing your steps is no longer an option. In fact, there's no such thing. Luckily, Tania tosses me a lifeline. And I would never let such a crucial opportunity pass me by. She decides to talk about something else.

"In your opinion, is Steve Jobs a genius or a nutjob?" she asks me.

"The inventor of Apple can't be anything but a genius."

"Did you know that when he was in college he went everywhere barefoot?"

"Everyone was a hippie back then."

"The truth is that in order to be a genius you have to be a little bit crazy."

"There are people who, the crazier they get, the stupider they are."

Tania nods and smiles a beautiful smile. As she heads off to take a shower, she gives me a nice French kiss. And, as I savor my breakfast of almond-flavored biscuits, I pick up the paper my mother left on the couch.

The front page is wreathed in clouds of glory. That asshole Enzo Laganà continues his triumphal march through the world of print journalism. An unstoppable trek toward success. This time I'm not alone, I'm arm-in-arm with the managing editor, Angelo Maritani. Our article is at the center of the page: A TORCHLIGHT MARCH AGAINST THE RAPISTS. I read the lede.

The reaction of the citizens of Turin hasn't been long in coming. It was, for that matter, practically inevitable. The rape of the Virgin of Via Ormea the day before yesterday can't just be filed away and forgotten. It should serve to awaken public opinion. That's the message that was hammered home by the torchlight march held yesterday in San Salvario. Meanwhile, the anger of the citizenry continues to swell. As of this writing, the two Roma still haven't been arrested. They're still at large, which just means they could easily strike again. The Roma community refuses to cooperate. Cont. on p. 2.

I turn to see the rest of the piece. There's just one short sentence about the burning of the trailer and the injuries to the woman and child. The details about the hooligans' violence have been downplayed. The one thing I know for sure is that this piece-of-shit article isn't the one I turned in to that asshole Maritani. And when he twisted my words, he pulled out all the stops. It would have been more ethical if he'd given himself the sole byline. None of this is my work. I'll demand an explanation; I don't like this way of doing things. I can't let them treat me like this—like some amateur or, even worse, some ignorant ass. I know about the stupid thing they call an "editorial line," but there's also a fucking journalistic code of ethics. We need to be honest and accurate. When the twisting of language and, above all, of facts reaches this level of unfairness, then it's time to denounce it for what it is: disinformation and propaganda. I see so many miniature Goebbelses all around me, little midgets who continue to mouth slogan after slogan: democracy, freedom of the press, freedom of speech, blah blah blah. To be perfectly honest with myself, I need to take some responsibility. No one, I repeat *no one*, forced me to choose journalism as a profession. I decided to become a journalist when I was still a university student majoring in sociology. Unfortunately, with the passage of time, I learned many things. First of all, our job isn't to inform the citizenry; it's to sell them a product called news, packaged within a very sophisticated and well-designed system that revolves around advertising. No newspaper, no television network, can live or survive without advertising. In all these years, especially in the past few, I've piled frustration on frustration, disappointment on disappointment. I've been held captive at a national newspaper's city desk. I thought that local reporting was the last surviving outpost of true journalism, but unfortunately I was wrong. I don't know how much longer I can go on like this. Sooner or later I'm going to have to make a decision. Something has to change if I don't want to die of boredom and regret.

I turn back to the front page. I glance at the editor in chief, Salvini's, editorial. The tune he's singing is clear from the headline alone: LET'S NOT CRIMINALIZE OUR CITIZENS. I dip in here and there.

The rape of the Virgin of Via Ormea is a very serious matter. This is the kind of thing that might happen during ethnic wars in Africa, but surely not here in our Turin, the first capital of the Italian state and the very emblem of the Italian boom and the economic miracle. How could this have happened? This is the question our citizens are insisting be answered. [. . .] Now is the time to say, without any beating around the bush: The situation is getting out of hand. Where are the public institutions? They can't go on pretending nothing is happening, ignoring the great emergency that is our lack of safety. [. . .] Our citizens are at their wits' end. And as we all know, when people are at their wits' end, they make mistakes, serious mistakes. The demonstration at the Roma camp is a worrisome sign, but it's also a clear message to the ruling class: Take steps immediately, before it's too late. This is the context within which we ought to read the news of the injuries inflicted upon the Roma woman and her son. A tragic turn of events, there's no doubt about that; but it certainly wasn't premeditated. Let's not criminalize our citizens.

Is any commentary required as far as the last of Salvini's observations is concerned? I think not. The editorial is crystal clear. Violence is justified, especially when it's inflicted on the weakest, those without a voice. I've thought often about the Roma, a people without a voice, with no right of rebuttal. The whole concept of the right of rebuttal needs to be analyzed, eviscerated, dismantled piece by piece. I'm reminded of the words of my friend Jean-Pierre, an anthropologist from Marseille: "If you want to understand any social, economic, or political phenomenon, concentrate on the relationships of power." He's perfectly right. Whoever holds the knife by the handle can do as he pleases. The mass media is a weapon at the disposal of the powerful, while the Roma, like other groups that are weak and enjoy no special protections, can only submit and accept the status quo. I really don't understand this Roma witch hunt. Why punish the entire Roma community simply because a single member of that community has committed a crime? Do we still believe in collective responsibility?

I'm sure of one thing. If anyone were to decide to make a couple of sound, commonsense statements about the Roma right now, he'd immediately be shouted down and denounced as a lily-livered liberal, accused of being a scaredy-cat, a card-carrying member of the "PC Police." This last designation is a true nugget, a genuine gem of a characterization. I remember well the first time I heard it. It was the end of the Nineties. I was working on a crime story, the murder of a husband and wife who owned a jewelry store Turin's city center. The murder was blamed on a gang of Albanians. In that case, too, a witch hunt against the Albanians and a move toward collective punishment swiftly followed. Against this chorus of opinion, one voice was heard: the voice of Don Costantino, a very courageous Turin priest. He tried to defend the Albanian community with a series of commensense statements, such as: "You can't tar them all with the same brush"; "Criminals form a small minority of the Albanian population"; "Belonging to a community can't be a crime." Unfortunately, hysteria is the number one enemy of common sense. The priest's words were, by and large, ignored. On that occasion, a city councilman described Don Costantino as "a card-carrying member of the PC Police." One week after the double homicide, the truth came out. The culprits weren't Albanian at all. It was a gang of Italian criminals. Of course, no one bothered to apologize to the Albanian community.

* * *

Editorial meetings are excruciatingly dull. Completely pointless. If you think it over carefully, they're only good for two things: On the one hand they create a little democratic facade, facilitate a pseudo freedom of speech, thanks to which everyone has the right to say some bullshit or other. On the other, they help to establish a sense of hierarchy. "We talk, we argue, we debate, but in the end someone has to have the final say": That's how Maritani dots the *i*'s in our meetings. And how can I disagree? Decisions are never made by committee. They're individual, the prerogative of whoever happens to be in charge, the ship's commander.

As we're amusing ourselves by shooting the journalistic shit, a young intern named Silvana (another victim of the system of disposable human resources?) comes in with a sheet of paper. Maritani makes no attempt to conceal his disapproval. The intern, though she knocked before entering, wasn't invited by anyone to take part in our little agora. The girl isn't stupid, quite the opposite. She's unruffled, she knows she has an ace up her sleeve. She speaks to Maritani, addressing him as "editor." Now a quick sidenote: I've never understood why the interns refer to him as the editor, and why he doesn't simply set them straight.

"Excuse me, Mr. Editor, I apologize for the intrusion."

"What is it? Can't you see we're having an editorial meeting?" says the fake editor in chief.

"I do see that, but you've always told us that wire reports wait for no one," the intern insists. She's very clever. She's going to have a brilliant career. Clever people have always played prominent roles in every field. Ours is no exception.

"That's a lesson no one should ever forget," Maritani says, self-satisfied, looking around at us and slipping into the guise of a guru surrounded by his disciples.

"Shall I read it?"

"Certainly. You have our attention."

"'Turin, 2:30 P.M. The girl from San Salvario, also known as the Virgin of Via Ormea, has changed her story. To the

Carabinieri who questioned her, she categorically denied she'd been raped. She stated that she'd had a consensual sexual experience, her first. She later panicked, fearful of how her family was likely to react. The girl from Turin has provided no further details. She did however say that she was very sorry. Her father has stated that the members of the family do not intend to speak to the press, in order to safeguard their privacy. This confession clears the Roma twins, who had been accused of rape, of all suspicion.' End of the wire report."

"This is certainly quite a bombshell," notes Maritani.

"It's not just a bombshell, it's a disgrace!" I burst out.

"We've had the wool pulled over our eyes big-time," Maritani adds.

"We've also played a part, and not an insubstantial one," I insist.

"Well, there's no point in crying over spilt milk now," Maritani cuts me off brusquely.

"No one is ever held to account in this country, as usual."

I begin a lengthy and quarrelsome dispute with Maritani in the presence of my fellow journalists, who observe the duel in silence. I remind him that I'd used the conditional in the first article I'd written, the day after the fake rape. He reiterates that the big boss is Salvini, certainly not him. And so if there are any criticisms, they should be addressed to the man in question. After a while I realize that we have no real chance of coming to an understanding, all we can do is trade accusations and blame. An editorial meeting is neither the time nor the place for a fair-minded discussion. We'd better stop now. I decide to head down to the café so I can relax with a nice hot espresso and an MS.

If Maritani wants to assuage his conscience and shift responsibility to others, Salvini first and foremost, that's his business. I can't do the same thing. I feel morally culpable. I should have dug in my heels and insisted on keeping the first article in the conditional. Instead, I let myself be treated worse than an intern, actually, worse than an ass.

What can we say about the young liar, the Virgin of Via Ormea? We have to admit that her performance was first-rate. A budding young actress. As for her nickname, I have a few objections. Instead of "virgin," we might do better to call her the "little saint" or perhaps the "good little virgin." Yes, the good little virgin of Via Ormea. Not bad. However it turns out, we have a spectacular piece of news: Via Ormea, notorious throughout Turin as the street of prostitutes and trannies, has also become the street of the virgins, or actually, of the false virgins.

As I leave the café, I try to buck myself up. I tell myself that this is the moment to fight back, to save what can be saved, to turn the situation on its head. Maybe the game isn't over yet. At least we can bring home a tie. To be defeated by the good little virgin really would be unacceptable. A true son of a bitch of an idea starts mosquitoing around in my ear.

* * *

I reach the home of the good little virgin. It's not crowded with people as it was last time. The gate is open, I don't bother to ring the buzzer. I knock at the door and Mauro, the father, opens it. He invites me in and shows me into the living room.

"Since this afternoon, we've been harrassed by journalists."

"They just want to know the truth," I comment.

"Listen, Enzo, I don't know how to apologize. We dragged you into this terrible story."

"I'm sorry, too."

"We don't know what we can do to repair the damage."

"Virginia has to clear things up."

"She already explained to the Carabinieri how things actually went."

"That's not enough, Mauro."

"What else are we supposed to do?"

"Clear things up as far the public opinion goes."

"How?"

"She has to give me an interview."

"No. Virginia is a wreck. We want to keep her at a safe distance from the press."

"But this is the only solution, believe me."

Mauro won't budge. He rejects the idea of the interview. I try to talk him into it, but it's no good. So I move on to Plan B and put my incredibly devious idea into motion.

"That means you're going to force me to show all my cards, Mauro."

"I don't understand you, Enzo."

"Virginia's life is in terrible danger."

"What are you talking about?"

"The Roma have sworn to take revenge."

My little charade works very well, not because it's solid and convincing, but because Mauro is exhausted. I explain to him that as a journalist I have a network of sources and informants (that part is true) and that I've learned through a Roma informant that the families from the burned camp have decided unanimously to take revenge (this part is obviously false). I throw in a long digression on the idea of the vendetta in the Roma tradition. I mix up concepts, throwing in honor, manliness, courage, truth, dignity, family—in other words, a giant heap of bullshit. In the end, I come to my conclusion: The Roma are willing to renounce their vendetta, but only in exchange for an apology, provided it's sincere and public.

I insist that the situation is very troubling. In brief, a diabolical mechanism has been set in motion, a time bomb. Metaphors are my strong suit. Metaphors are a magnificent linguistic stratagem. You can say everything and the opposite of everything. Let yourself be understood or misunderstood. What a mess, my friends. After these anthropological, linguistic, and metaphorical preambles, I arrive, right on schedule, at the core of my diabolical idea.

"The interview will help to defuse this bomb. You understand that, Mauro?"

"Bomb? I don't understand."

"It'll ward off their vengeance."

"How?"

"By making an apology, like I was saying."

My performance is magnificent. I manage to make a breach in his wall of mistrust. In the end he asks me to give him a couple of minutes to think it over. He wants to go talk to his daughter and wife. He's careful to insist that it's not going to be easy to talk them into it. So he's not promising a thing.

After a few minutes, Mauro comes back with his wife and daughter. I stand up to greet them. Virginia's eyes are red. She's cried and cried. She sits down next to her mother. From her initial silence I understand immediately that in order to get the orchestra to play, the conductor, that is, me, will have to tap his baton. A creative young man like myself certainly doesn't lack for can-do spirit. I start by reassuring them all.

"I'm here to help you," I begin.

"We've known you all our lives, Enzo," says the mother.

"We trust you. All of us in San Salvario are one big family," Mauro adds.

"Can you leave me alone with Virginia?" I ask the parents.

Mauro and his wife stare at me, astonished. They weren't expecting this request. But I've decided to go all in, and talking to her with her parents right there wouldn't do a bit of good. The good little virgin is a smart young thing. She has a vast imagination. Inventing a story about being raped and convincing everyone that it's true is no minor achievement. And what can we say about the notorious letter? "I forgive you! I forgive you! I forgive you!" Her parents acquiesce to my request and leave us alone.

Now I'm face-to-face with the good little virgin, very curious to learn the truth. I need to start in extremely cautiously; no rush, no false moves. My challenge is to get her to talk, and to do that I'll have to make use of all my experience.

I turn on the digital recorder.

"Listen, Virginia, I admire your courage."

"I'm not courageous."

"I mean that you had the courage to correct your mistake."

"I'm a coward."

"You could have gone on lying, but you didn't."

"How much more damage was I supposed to do?"

"But so far, you've only told a part of the truth. It's time to tell the whole truth now. Can I ask you a question?"

"Go ahead."

"Why did you accuse the two Roma?"

"I was afraid of what my family's reaction might be."

"Your father's?"

"No, my grandmother's."

"Your grandmother's?!"

The good little virgin's story begins with her grandmother. I don't remember where I once read that our destinies are all wrapped up in our names. Our names are born and die with us. They never leave us alone; there they are, printed on our IDs. They're tattoos, difficult to erase. Virginia! That's the name that her grandmother chose. Her grandmother not only chooses the names, she decides everything. It's her apartment. Her power is almost absolute. Virginity, for the grandmother and head of household, is an obsession. Every Christmas, since she was ten, Virginia has had to submit to the ritual of the oath: "I swear that I will remain pure until the day of my wedding." She swears the oath while looking at her grandmother and holding the bible in her hands. But the grandmother wasn't satisfied with the swearing of the oath. She's not the type to take much on faith. So they threw in a gynecological examination.

Once she had scientific proof, the grandmother could put her mind at ease. The good little virgin starts to cry. To make her stop, I go back to my questions.

"Why did you accuse the Roma?"

"I don't know, they popped into my mind . . ."

"Why them in particular?" I insist.

"I don't know."

"Do you hate them?"

"I'm no racist."

"Did you know the Roma twins?"

"Only by sight. I'd heard that they were expert burglars."

"Why did you accuse them instead of someone else?" I ask again.

The good little virgin has no answer. I don't think she's lying. She just dipped into the collective imagination. Simple as that. How can anyone forget the double murder that took place in Novi Ligure in 2001? Two teenagers, Erika and Omar, murdered Erika's mother and little brother and then blamed some Albanians. In the Nineties, the devils and witches were the Albanians, then, after September 11th, it was the Muslims, and then it was the Romanians' turn, and now it's the Roma. At the end of the confession, I can hardly waste my big opportunity.

"Who did you have sex with?"

"I can't say."

"Why not?"

"I just can't say. I'm sorry," she insists.

"Are you afraid of someone?"

"No, it's a secret. I haven't told anyone, not even my grand-mother and my parents."

There's no point in insisting. Unfortunately the big secret isn't about to be revealed. The question of all questions remains, at least for the moment, without an answer.

The good little virgin rebelled against her grandmother, not against her mother or father. A case for the psychologists and sociologists. I've always said it: Italy is a country for old people. They've always had the power here, and that's only becoming more and more true. The situation isn't likely to change anytime soon.

As I leave, I call my friend Luciano to inform him of the interview-slash-confession. I tell him that it'll come out in the next day's edition. It's one small thing pointing in the right direction: re-establishing the truth.

* * *

I go back to the newspaper. I shut myself up in my office. I'm pissed off at the world, especially at myself. I listen to the recording. I write without stopping, smoking one cigarette after another. I transcribe the good little virgin's account. I read it over a couple of times; I don't change much. I print it and I take a copy to Maritani.

After reading it over carefully, my managing editor picks up the phone and calls the big boss. He reads the confession out loud to him. After a brief exchange with Salvini he looks at me and says, in a calm, you might say in a slightly *too* calm voice:

"Nice job, Enzo, but we can't publish it in tomorrow's paper."

"Why not?"

"We need to take a minute to think it over."

"I don't understand."

"We don't want to make more mistakes."

"The young girl's story is a correction."

"That's not the way Salvini sees it."

"Either you publish my piece or I quit, Angelo," I say, exasperated.

"Enzo, don't be a horse's ass."

"I'd be a horse's ass if I stayed."

"All right. Let me try one more time with Salvini, but I can't promise you anything."

"Try to convince him."

I don't like extortion. But I don't have any other choice. I slam the door on my way out. I've been thinking about quitting for a while now. I'm not happy. If things go on like this, I'm liable to wreck my health. I often tell myself: It's time to quit. The situation's not going to improve. Am I pessimistic? No, not at all. I'm *very* pessimistic.

CHAPTER SIX
When you're playing with other people's money

There's no decision without a clean cut, there's no cut without pain, there's no pain without suffering. A chain of cause and effect. "Remember, Patrizia, making a choice is a painful thing," my psychoanalyst used to tell me over and over again. I was ready for a change. I was willing to run any risk. After many years I decided to stop. I couldn't go on. I was in bad shape, terrible shape. I raised the white flag.

During that period of malaise I did my best to hold out with all my strength. I employed various stratagems to bolster my morale, including cocaine, but nothing worked. The pressure just kept building. My job at the bank branch kept growing in importance. I was expected to persuade the savers, especially the small savers, to invest in our financial products. Not an easy job. I had to lie and lie well. What does it mean to lie well? You've got to play the part so as to arouse no suspicions. It's very important to be convincing. Pretend that you have the best interests of your clients at heart. Really, though, what you're trying to do is screw them. The script is always the same. And as often as not it took very little effort for me to attain my objective. I have to admit I was good at my job. My face inspired trust. Deep down, though, hid a giant unscrupulous asshole. I always began with the same phrase. It was bait, and it worked every time.

"You have money sitting useless in your account. It's a real shame," were the first words I spoke to my prey.

"What should I do?" my prey would always reply.

"You need to invest it."

"But I don't know anything about investing."

"That's why we're here."

"I don't trust the stock market."

"Who said anything about investing in the stock market?" I would reply, in a vaguely offended tone of voice.

People are afraid of the stock market and don't trust it; but they do trust the bank. In reality there is no difference whatsoever between the stock market and a bank. In both cases, it's people playing with other people's money. And in fact the source of the problem is precisely people's trust in banks. You should never, and I mean never ever, trust banks.

But nearly everyone falls for it. Out of greed or out of stupidity? "You need to make your money earn, and we offer safe financial products": This was the perfect bait. For example, it was super easy to sell shares in Parmalat before the collapse in 2003. All you had to do was repeat the same refrain: "As a commodity, milk is as solid as gasoline"; "The Italians are never going to give up their morning cappuccino"; "Milk is just like housing, the prices are always going to go up, they'll never drop."

The banks played a central role in the Parmalat collapse. They were the intermediaries and, most important, they were the guarantors. They'd call up savers to talk them into buying shares in Parmalat and other risky products by telling them fairy tales. We did everything we could to screw them, and we were tremendously successful. Then, once they were in the shit, we left them to their own devices. We washed our hands and our consciences both and never looked back.

Whoever said that the customer is king? I saw a fine ad recently that declared: The customer is president. There are no downsides when you're trying to decide whether you want to be king or president. All kidding aside, the customer, at least in our banks, is a child who can't do a thing without his legal guardian. We are legal guardians to an army of children. We do whatever we please. All they're expected to do is obey. Obviously, as is the way with children, every so often we tell them lies to keep them calm. For instance, we prefer the word "trust" to the word "obedience." "The financial product is one hundred percent safe, my dear child customer. Trust me." I was even willing to swear an oath if it meant they'd hand over their savings. Who could ever believe such bullshit? That a bank's financial product would be one hundred percent safe, absolutely risk-free? Well, the fact is that many customers did believe it, and they entrusted me with their cash. I often wondered whose fault that was. Are we guilty, the ones who do this shitty job, or are they? The law is on our side. Every time. We don't make a single move without signed authorization.

Banks are strange places. They're like houses of worship. When you go in, you check your rational mind at the door. That's why it's so easy to rip off the savers. A banker uses practically the same vocabulary as a priest, or an imam, or a rabbi, a language that consists by and large of promises. That's what we offer our customers: promises. The number-one promise is easy, risk-free profit. But there's a big difference: Priests and other religious authorities promise paradise in the next world, while bankers guarantee heaven on earth. Maybe that's what pushes the customers to tumble so easily into our trap.

Personally, I love to imagine money parked like so many cars. It's a very easy metaphor to explain and, above all, to understand. If you have a car and you leave it parked in the garage, after a while it just won't start. It's like a human being; it needs to move. Money loves to move. Money likes to get out and do sports, go dancing, take trips.

Money needs to move. All the time. That's the first rule. The second rule is that there are only a few winners (always the same) and lots of losers, tons in fact. The situation has always been the same. Why? Money doesn't grow, it just changes location—hands, wallet, bank account, etc. Money doesn't like to be lonely, it likes to hang out in large groups, become capital, power, force.

I have to admit that I've screwed over lots and lots of small savers. Their only fault? They trusted me. My only job was to get their money. All that matters are results; methods are of no importance. And if I was going to perform my professional duties and earn my salary, there were a couple of rules I needed to keep in mind. First and foremost, never look anyone in the eye. These are all customers, nothing more. So it's pointless, in fact it's actually harmful, to feel pity or compassion for a retiree or a little old lady. These are people who've decided to invest their damn savings. That's all that matters, nothing else. Second, never listen to your conscience, I mean your moral conscience, the one that might make you suddenly develop misgivings when you're face-to-face with a customer.

After so many years, my conscience had fallen into a deep sleep. It took years and years to wake it back up. Then one client turned my life upside down: old Signora Giacometti. I'd known her for a long time. I persuaded her to invest in a worthless financial product and of course she lost everything.

"I don't have anything left," she told me, sobbing.

"I'm sorry to hear that, Signora."

"I trusted you." She used the informal with me, she thought of me as a granddaughter.

"It's not my fault," I retorted.

"Whose fault is it then?"

"The system's, Signora."

"What is this system, anyway?" she asked me, drying her eyes.

"Something that's bigger than us."

It's wonderful to put all the blame on the system. The blessed system. But the system is us. The poor old thing went away sadder than before. I was about to tell her that the blame was hers. That she shouldn't have even trusted yours truly. The system is pitiless. The bank is a machine that's gone crazy, that cares only about profits. It doesn't give a hoot about little old ladies and small savers.

But Signora Giacometti had her revenge. She found an ingenious way of making me pay. In fact, if we'd been two boxers, I'd have said she delivered a knockout.

* * *

I can't remember exactly when and where I met Medina. Maybe it was in the summer, near Piazza San Carlo. I often took my lunch hour in that area. There were coffee breaks, too, at least three a day, with the inevitable caffè macchiato. I can't afford those anymore. Only rarely do I set foot in a café. Since I'm a gypsy, they ask me to pay in advance and they watch me suspiciously. Before, all the baristas treated me with kid gloves. Those were other times. Now they see me as a potential thief per the theory: All gypsies are thieves. A rule that admits of absolutely no exceptions, no point in trying to challenge it. *Vox populi, vox Dei.*

The smile! That's what struck me the first time I saw Medina. She asked me for a coin. I gave her a euro. Then I kept seeing her. Every time, a euro. For her it was a kind of reliable income and for me an agreeable ritual.

My encounter with Medina wasn't easy. She struck a chord deep in my being, touched a raw nerve to do with my vision of the world. I was struck by her physical appearance—not her clothing, but the total absence of makeup. How can a woman leave the house without a trace of makeup on? I have to admit that this question has tormented me for a long time. I was convinced, like most women, that makeup was a form of clothing. Maybe the truest form of clothing. Can you go around naked? Blessed makeup! And why is it called that? Because it's made up, not authentic. How much time I wasted every morning making myself up. And I was never satisfied. To say nothing of the cost. I spent almost half of my salary on my appearance. A money pit.

I even hired an image expert. That's no longer something only people in show business and politics do. In our business the idea of an "attractive presence" is fundamental. It carries weight on your resume. A career requires sacrifices of all kinds. What worried me most were the signs of aging. I waged a relentless battle against wrinkles. I was willing to do anything to get them off my face. I relied on cosmetic surgery, it was crucial. Luckily I stopped in time, before plunging into the abyss of facelifts and Botox. I limited myself to minor, noninvasive interventions, just to smooth out the crow's feet around my eyes. Now, praise the Lord, I'm free of all that. I don't even think about it anymore. And when I do, I tell myself I was an insecure fool.

When I worked in the bank I learned a great many things: A lack of security, for instance, is a huge problem. When people feel insecure, they fall into lots of traps. They become easy to rip off. It doesn't take much, and the job is done. Lack of security is a huge flaw; it's like a cancer that destroys the body from within. It's hard to win a battle when the enemy is a part of you. In brief, because you're insecure, you're forced to fight a sort of civil war.

Since I became a gypsy, I have more self-confidence. It might seem strange, but it's true. I've changed my priorities. Makeup and clothing are no longer indispensable. Those are accessories, they can help to fight insecurity exactly the way prescription drugs do, tranquilizers first and foremost. There are other things that matter more in life. For instance, being able to look at yourself in the mirror without fleeing from the sight of your face. Yes, I've started making peace with myself, loving myself the way I am. I can say that I've saved the money

I would have spent on a psychoanalyst. In other words, I've done my own therapy, relying on my own resources. And it wasn't long before I was seeing results.

One thing I'm very proud of has to do with colors. As a gypsy, I've truly enjoyed myself with the color yellow, which I'm crazy about, along with white. Yellow is a color that's looked down upon, viewed with contempt, and I've never understood why. Since the rules say that you have to dress not the way you like, but the way others like, I've censored myself for years. Now I dress mainly in yellow, and I don't care what people think. The thing that really matters to me is being comfortable. There are people who've started to call me "the Yellow Gypsy" or "the Gypsy in Yellow." But I prefer my own name, or nickname: Drabarimos.

My friendship with Medina has grown stronger over time. We started talking more often. She speaks a very basic Italian—she more or less makes herself understood and she understands the essence of what you tell her. She has a limited vocabulary, but she manages to transmit force and passion with her words. She often gesticulates, and so she is able to speak with her hands, her head, her eyes, and her lips. Her great strength is her smile, which easily becomes a lovely laugh, an infectious one that's practically impossible to resist.

At the beginning of our friendship, I was slow to let myself go. That's how I am by nature. That's why I've never had many friends, male or female. It's not easy for me to trust people and open up to others. Medina is very different, she's a river in flood. When she starts talking she doesn't stop. And so, before long, I knew all there was to know about her. She's twenty-two, though she looks about ten years older. I wouldn't have bet a single euro on her real age. It was practically impossible to guess with any confidence. She told me that she was married and already had two children. She talked very little about her husband. She said that he spent more time in prison than with her. They were married at a very young age in order to honor an agreement between the two families. Everyone knows that it's pointless to talk of love when a marriage is arranged.

I noticed that Medina's story changed every time she told it. She'd add and subtract details as the situation or mood struck her. One time she told me that she'd been orphaned as a small child, but later she talked about her parents, who still live in Romania. Another time she told me that she came from a large family, but not long afterward she said that she was an only child, just like me. I've always overlooked these details. I think that we all have the sacrosanct right to say or not say whatever we like. Only the Inquisition was obsessed with the absolute truth. Which explains their reliance on torture. Medina wasn't lying, she was acting. That's all. In short, since she had to play a role, she was necessarily obliged to adjust the facts and twist reality. In my life, I've learned that truth is a difficult thing, never perfect. It has plenty of flaws, plenty of dark spots. Lies, in the final analysis, are useful in tidying up the disorder and organizing the whole.

Medina's versions of the truth changed as our relationship solidified. One day she looked at me and told me: "Now you've become a friend, a true girlfriend. True girlfriends are sisters. From now on, I'll only tell you the truth." Medina has remained faithful to her promise. Since that day, she's never once changed her account of her life. And the last version of her truth is that she has two small children, Demir and Zafira. Her husband is a criminal who's serving out a prison sentence. Her parents are alive and well and still live in Romania. She'd like to bring them over but the current situation makes that impossible.

I've tried to help her in various ways. I had closets full of clothes, and when I gave her outfits she was very pleased. She went and sold them at the Balùn, the secondhand market at Porta Palazzo. Every so often she'd ask me to read certain documents. She's illiterate, she's never set foot in a school. I still can't understand how she can live without knowing how to read and write. Maybe writing isn't so fundamental after all, maybe we can do without. But how does she find her way in train stations, how does she learn the schedules and the platforms? What does she do about street names?

* * *

Presentiments are real, they do exist. I can't explain this rationally, but I'm sure of it. It's a sort of warning that comes to you from within. An inner voice that puts you on guard, tells you to get ready because something serious or dangerous is about to happen. In this context you might call it a sixth sense. This thought about presentiments occurred to me when I saw that enraged mob descending on our camp.

It all happened very fast. Around 7:30 P.M. we heard voices coming closer. At first it seemed like sound coming from a radio or a television set, but in fact it was an actual demonstration. A big demonstration; and what they were protesting against was us.

We shut up our trailers and went away to watch from a distance. There were lots of people with candles and signs of all kinds. I didn't have a chance to read them all, but it only took a few to make me realize that there was trouble in the air: "Get the Gypsies Out of Turin"; "Gypsies=Rapists"; "Get Out, Rapists"; "Down with Bleeding-Heart Liberals"; "Get the Rapists away from Our Little Girls"; "Enough with Urban Blight."

We immediately understood the gravity of the situation. The tension increased as the demonstrators got closer to the camp. At a certain point, two guys with their faces hidden behind helmets broke off from the main group and headed for Medina's trailer. Then and there we didn't know what they were planning to do. But after a few seconds we saw them pouring liquid around the trailer. Medina started screaming: "Demir! There's a little boy inside! Demir! Demir! Demir!"

The little boy had secretly gone back into the trailer to get his favorite toy. The bastards had used gasoline or some other highly flammable substance. Just like that, the trailer was on fire. I couldn't believe my eyes. Medina ran toward the trailer and I ran after her shouting in anger and despair: "Stop! Stop!" Medina was afraid, she was hesitating. But I didn't think twice; I ran straight in, despite the flames.

I only remember a few scenes. I enter the trailer, I hear the little boy crying. I pick him up and take him in my arms. I feel the fire on my flesh. I rush out and I fall. Then I can't hear anything else . . . total silence!

I wake up with a start; someone is banging insistently at my door. Tania keeps sleeping. The first thought that occurs to me as I go to open the door is that it could be my dear mother. Maybe she lost or forgot her house key somewhere. That's never happened before. But sooner or later, at least once in a lifetime, these things do happen. After all, my mamma, alias Mrs. I Do, is a human being. All the same, these hypotheses are filed away the very instant I open the door. Luckily the suspense doesn't last long.

"Can you tell me what this is?"

"It's a newspaper."

"No, as far as I'm concerned it's a piece of shit."

"Fine. It's a piece of shit, if that makes you happy. Do you want to fight it out here on the landing or inside?"

After a few seconds of hesitation, Luciano comes in. We sit down in the living room. He throws the newspaper on the sofa, snorting theatrically. I try to stay calm. That's not going to be easy. I know keeping my temper is going to be quite a challenge—no, a trying ordeal. What the hell, I just woke up. I haven't even had a chance to wash my face. I haven't had an espresso yet, I haven't smoked my first cigarette. In short, I'm a public menace. I can avail myself of the right to remain silent, or plead an inability to distinguish right from wrong and hope for leniency (in case I wind up committing a murder).

The truth is that I don't feel like arguing. Why not? I'm an easygoing guy and I don't want to wake up Tania. I can't afford to forget about my mother and Aunt Quiz, who are right around the corner. They could show up here any minute. My apartment is next door to Aunt Quiz's. You can hear everything. I close the door to the living room. I try not to respond to Luciano's provocations. I pick up the newspaper and I take a glance at the front page. I don't see any Enzo Laganà. Where did my story on the good little virgin of Via Ormea end up?

"What the fuck are you looking for?" shouts Luciano.

"The confession."

"It's not there."

"Those bastards!"

"You made a fool out of me," he says, still shouting.

"I turned it in yesterday after calling you," I assure him.

"Then they screwed you over, big-time."

"It's time for you to calm the hell down, Luciano."

I realize that the situation could quickly get out of hand. I'm a pretty even-tempered guy, but once I see red, there's no holding me back. It's bad news for everyone. I make a tremendous effort to keep from losing the bet I made with myself and flipping out. So I concentrate on the damn newspaper, perusing it carefully, but I find nothing. Not a trace of the good little virgin's confession. Threatening to resign didn't do a bit of good. There are two options: Either Maritani was unable to persuade Salvini or else he just pretended to try, making a fool out of me. I'm inclined towards option number two. Better to trust no one. Being suspicious of everyone and everything isn't paranoia; in fact, it's a wonderful quality, worth cultivating always and everywhere. A sort of self-defense, a vaccination against being screwed over by the first guy you come across.

I turn back to the front page. My eyes light on the editor in chief's editorial. Impossible to miss. The headline is in the grand tradition of self-criticism: WE SINCERELY APOLOGIZE. Salvini and sincerity? That's like the devil and holy water. This "sincerely" just pisses me off even more. I read bits of it here and there as Luciano lights a cigarette, paying no heed to the duties of a guest. Normally there's no smoking in this apartment when Tania's around. She's a health nut. But now's not the time to nitpick. Right now, the number one priority is to calm down this erupting volcano known as Luciano Terni.

The story of the young Turinese girl, the Virgin of Via Ormea, has taken an unexpected turn. Yesterday, she changed her account. She dropped all accusations against the two Roma boys. We can't fail to acknowledge the courage of this young girl and her family. Admitting a mistake is an act of courage and great honesty. The innocence of the two Roma doesn't mean that the Roma problem has now been solved and no longer exists. Please, let's not kid around. The real trap is that laid by bleeding-heart liberals. Their brand of politics is the real disease that's afflicting our country. [. . .] For our part, we want to admit our mistake. Let's call it an oversight, a distraction, mere carelessness. We wrote an unfortunate headline in the aftermath of the announcement of the fake rape. We had no way to know the truth. We were deceived, just as public opinion was. [. . .] In short, these are the risks of our wonderful profession. We'd now like to apologize to our readers and ourselves. We promise that we'll take great care in the future to avoid ever making similar mistakes. We care a great deal about sincerity, honesty, and professionalism.

"Do you like the editorial your editor in chief wrote?" Luciano asks, piling on.
"It's disgusting."
"The last section made me want to throw up," he adds.
"I'm going to hand in my resignation today."
"It's easy to leave a sinking ship."
"What the fuck do you want from me?"

Luciano wasn't expecting my decision. He'd come to let off steam, but unfortunately he picked the wrong person. Salvini's bullshit at the end includes some real pearls. How can you apologize to your readers and to "ourselves"? And say nothing to the actual victims, that is, the Roma? The true injured party. How can you apologize to yourself? It's sheer madness. In this piece of shit paper, however, there is at least one piece of good news: The police have arrested two soccer hooligans and charged them with the arson at the Roma camp. But they'll be released as soon as possible. At this point, we've scraped the bottom of the bottom of the barrel. I can't keep doing this disgusting job and working for this impossibly screwed up newspaper. It's time to throw in the towel. It's taken me too long to make up my mind. As far as this story about the good little virgin goes, I feel like an accomplice. I put in my fair share. Bravo, Enzo! I don't see any substantial distinction between outright guilt and complicity. These are just semantic nuances. The fundamentals are the same.

Suddenly something happens that defies every explanation, defies every script, defies imagination, even. Luciano starts to cry. I realize immediately that this is no playacting. It's all damnably real. I've never seen him like this. He really catches me off guard. Holy shit, I just woke up. I haven't had my coffee or my cigarette. My poor brain can't work without its full tank of gas. I don't know how much longer I can hold out. How can I hang tough?

"This is an injustice," he says in a thin voice.

"You're right. I'm really sorry."

"No people on earth have suffered as grievously as mine," he adds.

"Your people?! I don't understand, Luciano."

"I'm a Rom, Enzo."

"You are?!"

"Yes, I'm a Rom, a Piedmontese Sinti."

"What are you talking about?"

Luciano reveals to me the secret that he's kept hidden for twenty years. He discovered that he was a Piedmontese Sinti by chance. During his grandmother's funeral he saw a number of strange rituals: Pockets and buttons were opened and unhooked, pocket handkerchiefs were checked to make sure there were no knots in them, a knot in the nightshirt she was wearing was untied, the window was immediately opened, shoes were put on her feet, her cane was put by her side, and a coin was placed first on her forehead, and then in her pocket. After much insistent questioning, his father took him aside and told him the truth. At first he refused to believe it, but then, as the years went by, he began to understand his roots and, with some difficulty, to accept them. But he'd never had the courage to say it publicly. He was ashamed. Now I understand his commitment to the cause of immigrants' rights. The Roma have always played a major role in his work as a volunteer and a political activist. It isn't easy to accept certain truths. It takes time, and you have to work hard on yourself. To acknowledge your own roots is a complicated task. The Piedmontese Sinti have a thoroughly Italian history. They arrived in Piedmont in the Middle Ages, so we can say that they're Italian, in fact, *italianissimi*, but only in theory. In reality, they're foreigners in their own homeland. People still look at them as gypsies, and only as gypsies.

I listen to Luciano in silence. I have nothing to say, and he certainly doesn't need to hear my immediate reactions. We'll have time to calmly resume our discussion later on. Now he needs to talk; he needs to let the cat out of the bag.

"You know what the hardest thing is, Enzo?"

"What?"

"The shame . . ."

"These things take time."

"More than time, it takes a lot of courage."

"A bastard like you can hardly be short on courage," I say, trying to ease the tension.

Luciano acknowledges the gesture with a fleeting smile. He tells me about the fire at the Roma camp, the injured little boy who could have been his son, the wounded woman he knew very well; he tells me her name too, though I don't commit it to memory. He feels fully involved. He knew these people. They're people who are trying to survive in spite of a thousand hardships. The biggest obstacle they face is rejection. The Roma are rejected a priori. They can do all the good they want in the world, but in the eyes of the people they will always be nasty and dirty, thieves and criminals. What's the point of behaving well, being polite, courteous, and eager to help out? What good is it to extend the hand of friendship when no one will take it? Why bother to smile when others just look away? It's no way to live. "I've never seen people as terrorized as the Roma," Luciano says over and over again, drying his tears. "They live in a state of absolute vulnerability. They live day by day, like birds of passage. No permanent abode, here today and gone tomorrow."

As I listen to Luciano, I realize what it means to be wounded in one's soul and in one's memory. I don't know if there's a cure, but one thing's for sure: His pain is enormous. Obviously, the wounds of the body are easier to heal because you can see and touch them. The wounds of the soul and the memory, on the other hand, form invisible scars. You can't see them, but you can feel them all the time.

I go into the kitchen to get him a glass of water. When I get back I find Luciano on his feet. He wants to leave. He comes over to me and, without a word, gives me a hug. A powerful hug, long and silent.

"I apologize, Enzo."

"You don't need to apologize. I'm just sorry for this whole mess."

"You're a real friend, right?"

"Are you saying you have some doubts, asshole?!" I say, trying to drag a smile out of him.

"Promise me this, that you won't go around telling people that you saw me cry."

"You think I'm a big enough idiot to miss out on an opportunity like that?"

In the end, I succeed. Luciano lets loose with a fine laugh. We agree to see each other again very soon.

* * *

That afternoon Sam calls me up, he wants to see me about something urgent. We meet at Valentino Park. Stretching my legs does me good. I need some fresh air. I feel as if I'm suffocating. I'd like to leave, right now. Going to the mountains with Tania would be a nice solution. But I have to wait for the thunderstorm known as the good little virgin to pass. So far, we've all felt the consequences. What a wreck!

As usual, Sam shows up half an hour late. A Mediterranean habit, some might say. Respect for time isn't part of our culture, our manners, our vision of the world. I think it's a form of vendetta. You can't confront time face-to-face; it disrespects and offends everyone, without exception. It always escapes us. So how can we respect someone who always treats us rudely? A tooth for a tooth, and go fuck yourself.

Sam guesses at my state of mind. You don't need a degree in psychology or the ability to read minds to figure it out. I'm down, my batteries are drained. I'm stressed out. I really don't feel like working. But the asshole never passes up a chance; he really knows how to poke at me.

"Bellezza is going around telling people that you're his newest recruit."

"Really?"

"He says that you're his man, at least as far as the media goes."

"Why don't you both go fuck yourselves?"

"It's not very nice to talk that way about your new master."

"Do me a favor and stop busting my chops."

"Come on, Enzo, I'm just kidding."

"This isn't the time for it."

Sam realizes that wisecracks are off limits today. My level of tolerance is at a historic low. It's been quite a while since I've felt like this. There's a great anger inside me. I don't know whether I'll be able to control it. It seems like an untamable beast. When you take into account my two forms of exhaustion—physical and mental—it's hard to start swimming again. I risk drowning the minute I plunge into the water.

"What's wrong, Enzo?"

"Tomorrow I'm handing in my resignation at the paper."

"Have you thought this through?"

"I can't go on, Sam."

"Is this because of the fake rape?"

"Let's just say that that's the straw that broke the camel's back."

Sam is a very particular kind of guy. He seems like someone you can't count on at all, someone with his head in the clouds, but there are moments when he turns into a different person. He listens to you carefully and he helps you to think things through if you're confused. I talk to him for a long time, and he doesn't interrupt me much. I tell him about the enormous frustration and disenchantment I'm feeling with my work as a journalist. I feel like the idiot sheep in the flock. There's a narrow path you're supposed to follow. And you can't wander off it.

In our journalistic jargon, this blessed path goes by a very specific name: editorial line. What does that mean? It's quite simple. The owner or owners of the newspapers (they might also be called majority shareholders) make the weather. A

newspaper resembles a military base. When the upper eche-
lons make a decision, it immediately becomes an order to be
obeyed. For example, when the high command decides to go
to war, it's the enlisted men who actually do the fighting and
dying. If they emerge victorious, then the praise and medals go
to the top brass. I feel like a miserable private being sent out to
fight someone else's war. In the end there's only one way out,
and that's to leave, slamming the door behind you, to desert.
To save yourself before it's too late.

"I understand your reasons, but I'd suggest taking a little
time."

"What good would that do?"

"A good decision is the fruit of a clear mind. Wait at least a
week, then see how you feel," he insists.

"By the way, what did you want to talk to me about?"

"My visa. Can you rehire me as your domestic employee?"

"Are you asking me to be your boss again?"

"We say employer, not boss."

"I like boss."

Sam still manages to make me smile. Though this visa thing
is a real ball and chain. I met Sam in 1998, when he was still
without papers. After four years as an undocumented alien, I
hired him as a housekeeper so he could get his visa, though he
paid his own withholdings.

As soon as he had his visa, he asked me to fire him. It's the
only time in my life I've hired someone and then fired him. I
can see that it's not going to be the last time. "Firing" is an ugly
word. I felt like a worm even though I knew it was all a farce.
I grew up with a father who had a job at Fiat. The battles the
union fought were a part of my political education. In any case,
even though Sam is officially a domestic worker, as indicated
on his papers, he's unofficially an artist. Unfortunately, he still
hasn't made it big as a musician.

"Well, Enzo, what do you say?"

"I accept, but on one condition."

"I'm listening."

"You have to come clean my house three times a week, without pay."

"What do you take me for? Some kind of slave?"

"I have to protect myself. They might decide to investigate and see if you actually work for me."

"You're an asshole."

"Take it or leave it."

"You're a piece of shit, a heartless exploiter."

"That's no way to talk to your future boss."

"In the end you're worse than Bellezza."

"Well, now he's my idol!"

After kidding around, we work out the details: the documents to be compiled, the various deadlines. By now we can claim considerable expertise in this field. I should point out that the immigration laws are riddled with holes. If an immigrant wants to renew his visa, the poor guy has to prove that he has a more or less open-ended employment contract. But where is he supposed to find such a thing?

These days, contracts like that are a vanishing species. Not even us Italians can find them. The poor immigrants have to figure out a workaround. How? By buying one, which means paying a fake employer and then also paying their own withholdings. The alternative is to ask a goodhearted friend to volunteer, someone like yours truly, willing to run a risk on their behalf.

* * *

I invite Tania out to dinner. I try to make her forget about our vacation in the mountains. On our way to the restaurant, we run into Mario Bellezza. I'd have avoided him if I could, but there was no way. It strikes me that he's starting to be like dog poop in San Salvario: it's really hard to make it through a week without stepping in some at least once. In my head, I apologize to the dogs. "It's not that the dogs are rude, it's their owners." I'm reminded of the careful distinction made by my childhood friend Irene Morbidi, the most famous animal rights activist in Piedmont. Now that I think about it, wouldn't it be a good idea to entrust neighborhood watches with the task of solving the dog-poop problem? They could keep an eye out for and fine the rude owners. Now that's a good suggestion, and one we should implement immediately.

With Mario Bellezza, alias Beerbelly, you have to be on your guard. It's the easiest thing in the world to fall into his trap. In order to win, you have to make sure you don't go along with his tactics. I won't give him the chance to increase the level of negativity. My threshold of tolerance has been breached. This time, I want to change the rules of the game. Yes, I try to stop playing defense. Let's see what a counterattack can do. To hell with the *catenaccio*, the back-line strategy based on fear of the opponent and boredom. Hooray for total soccer, which is all showmanship, fun, and lots and lots of goals.

"Did you enjoy our good little virgin's show?"

"They're just kids!" he replies.

"Always justifying yourself. No self-criticism."

"She fucked up, let's call it a prank," he insists.

"Ruining a bunch of people's lives is just a prank?!"

"There are worse things in the world, my dear Enzo."

"I don't see what could be worse than a little boy seriously hurt because someone else had sex," I put in.

"The girl made a mistake."

"We should all be ashamed of ourselves."

"My conscience is clear."

"Oh, really?"

"Yes."

"Well, lucky you."

Bellezza tries to persuade me. In life, everything has a positive side and a negative side. Like a coin with two faces. For example, the fire and the wounding of the Roma were collateral damage. Certainly, no one should ever rejoice over other people's misfortunes. But at least one good thing's come out of all this: The gypsies and their encampment are both gone. We risked seeing Valentino Park, one of the most beautiful parks in all of Europe, transformed into a camp for nomads. Why shouldn't we feel satisfied at least in part? The gypsies took to their heels, like rats after a successful extermination. Public opinion is finally engaged in the debate over the lack of security in our cities. We've given our political class, which is incapable of solving problems, a fine lesson. The important thing is to take action. Always. If you make a mistake, that doesn't matter. Bellezza sums everything up. And so, now that all's said and done, every cloud has a silver lining. Tania, who usually stays out of my discussions with Bellezza, emerges from her silence.

"It's not nice to talk about the Roma as if they were rats," Tania objects.

"You have a point. It's an insult to the rats. If you ask me, gypsies aren't human beings," Bellezza says, piling on.

"What are you saying?" Tania asks, unwilling to let this go.

"I mean that they don't behave the way we human beings do," he clarifies.

"Unacceptable words. You're a racist," Tania snaps.

"I'm no racist, I'm just defending my neighborhood."

"You should be ashamed of yourself," my girlfriend replies.

"Why should I be ashamed of myself?! You're lucky that you're Swedish. In all of Sweden you have only one gypsy, and he actually helps your national team win its matches," Bellezza lobs back.

"Sweden?! We only have one gypsy?! What are you talking about? I don't understand." Tania glances at me, confused.

"The gypsies are like us. We southerners were treated the same way," I say, coming to Tania's aid.

"What do southerners have to do with this, Enzo!" says Bellezza, annoyed.

"They have everything to do with it!" I say brusquely.

We decide to end this discussion with Bellezza. We leave without even saying "ciao." Tania is very angry. I do my best to calm her down, but it's not easy. To start with, I explain Bellezza's idiotic comment about Sweden. First of all, since she's a real blonde, and really blond, she's automatically Swedish. That's just the way our blessed Italian imagination operates. There's nothing we can do about it. That's how things have always been, that's how they are, and that's they're going to stay. It just takes patience and, of course, a healthy dose of resignation. Then I clear up the reference to the "Swedish gypsy" who is the pride and joy of his country's national team. He's talking about the star athlete Zlatan Ibrahimović, who used to play for Juventus and is now with Barcelona. There's a rumor going around that he's of Roma origin. I think that's only said to insult and offend him. To many people, being called a gypsy is the worst possible insult. I remember that years ago the ex-striker Bobo Vieri was called a gypsy because he changed team every year. A nomadic soccer player. He, too, wore the Juventus jersey.

"I still don't understand. Can I ask you a question?" Tania asks.

"Go ahead."

"How come this asshole still hasn't been arrested for inciting racial hatred?"

"Now that's a good question," I reply, stalling for time so I can think it through.

Actually, there's very little to say. To be perfectly honest, I don't have an answer. So I clutch at theories like a drowning man. Fuck it, I can't get by with just an "I don't know." My thought is that here in Italy, but maybe elsewhere too, the weakest are forced to submit to a tidal wave of insults and injuries, and they're not able to hit back. It's the law of the strongest. I remind Tania of a great Maghrebi fable I read years ago. Once upon a time there was a young peasant who wanted to become a barber. To realize his dream he needed to practice a lot, but there was a problem: No one was willing to trust him to cut their hair. So he turned to the village wise man, who suggested he start by cutting orphans' hair. Why? Because nobody cared about the poor orphans. To be perfectly blunt: The orphans had no protectors. The moral of the fable is clear: We live in a world made up of protectors and the protected, masters and servants, bosses and underlings. In short, something of a jungle.

"So as far you're concerned, the Roma are like the orphans in the fable."

"That's right," I say, confirming my theory.

"But this is 2010, Enzo!" she retorts, a hint of despair in her voice.

"That doesn't change anything," I insist.

The passage of time does nothing to ensure progress, improvement, and happiness. I let myself move into the realm of sociological reflections. I mean, I'm proud of my degree in sociology. I have all the credentials I need to make my point. Certain forms of human behavior remain unchanged over time. For instance: injustice, bullying, and abuse. The unmistakable proof of my point of view is war. Mankind, in spite of modernity, technology, prosperity, democracy, human rights, and so on and so forth, has never managed to repudiate war. Why not? Because inside every human being there lives an animal that will never be domesticated. That's the way we are. We can't be fixed. In other words, to put it in the simplest terms: we're well and truly screwed! Is there anything left for us to try? No. I'm sorry. Tania remains confused, she doesn't subscribe to my point of view.

"You're too much of a pessimist, my love."

"I'm a realist," I explain.

"But that means you have no faith in the world, in mankind."

"It's not a matter of faith, Tania."

"What point is there in living without faith?!"

"The term 'living' is a bit of an exaggeration."

"Than what would you call this?"

"Surviving."

"Really?"

"Just as it is for the Roma," I say, coming full circle with my pearls of wisdom.

Tania has nothing left to say. Perhaps she simply can't understand this reality—to call it surreal truly is an understatement—or else she's just bored. Poor Tania. She came to Turin to relax, thinking she'd get to have a good time in the mountains with her sweetheart. Instead she finds herself forced to witness a nauseating and shameful spectacle, acted out by players both stupid and hypocritical. Could you ever imagine a Finnish version of the good little virgin? And what about Bellezza? There's no one like him anywhere else on earth. He truly is "DOC," clearly "Made in Italy"! The envy of who knows how many other nations, eh?

CHAPTER EIGHT
When I grow up, what I want to be is happy

As time passed, the bank became everything to me. One night, I had a dream, and of course it couldn't have been set anywhere other than inside the walls of a bank. It's one of the first dreams I had when I first started going to my psychoanalyst. There's a mouse in my bank's branch office. My colleagues are interested in him. Apparently they're betting money on whether or not he's going to make it. They're all rooting one way or the other and they're very excited. The scene is reminiscent of an underground fighting ring. The mouse is hungry, terribly hungry. In front of him is an open safe and in it is a little piece of cheese. To get to it, the mouse has to get past an obstacle, a big fire. He's struggling, hesitant. One step forward, another step back.

"So what did you decide to do in the end, Patrizia?" the psychoanalyst asked me.

"Me?"

"Of course. The mouse is you."

"What do you mean it's me?"

"Don't try to hide."

"I'm not trying to hide."

"Come out into the open. Go on, answer the question."

"The mouse goes through the fire and gets to the piece of cheese."

"Good job, Patrizia."

"But she gets burnt," I concluded despairingly, and started to cry.

That day the psychoanalyst explained to me that hunger is a reference to greed, to one's career, to one's job. The mouse is small and alone and that's how I felt, deep down. The mouse is my shadow. In the bank, I have no protection. No one will help the mouse to get through the fire; in fact, they're betting against him. For them, it's all just a game, while for him it's a matter of survival, of life or death. The ending is very significant: The mouse makes it to the cheese but he also gets burned. I don't believe there's a more atrocious death than being burned alive.

Loneliness is the first step toward both suicide and depression. My biggest problem is that I was alone while surrounded by others: colleagues, friends, travel companions, shopping partners, gym buddies. I learned at my own expense that the deepest loneliness isn't being alone, but feeling alone.

And yet for my career I was willing to damn my soul. The further ahead I went, the more I met with cross fire. Obviously there were always twice as many obstacles for a woman. I had to show my claws to make headway. I was a tiger in the middle of the jungle. I fought with every ounce of strength I possessed to consolidate my position in the branch office. Twenty years of my life sacrificed to my career, to the goddess of success. The question I ask myself today is: Was it worth it? All things considered, what do I have to show for it? Nothing, except for a sea of internal tempests! At a certain point, I seriously thought I was going to come down with a tumor. I was truly frightened.

What's the point of working hard and making so many sacrifices if it doesn't make you happy? Shouldn't happiness be the barometer we use to gauge and evaluate our actions? I remember that back in elementary school there was a very strange little girl, Antonia, I never forgot her name. In response to the supremely stupid question children are asked the world over—"What do you want to be when you grow up?"—some of us said doctor, policeman, lawyer, soldier. Of course, we all changed professions all the time. Only Antonia always said the same thing: "When I grow up, I want to be happy." The teacher's explanations were all in vain. Being happy isn't a profession, a job, a career. But she was unswerving. She wanted to be happy, and that was that. I think Antonia was right. "Take wisdom from the mouths of fools and children," says a beautiful Arabic proverb.

Becoming happy ought be the finest profession on earth. I would welcome hard work and sacrifices for any cause as noble as that. Happiness is as contagious as optimism and cheerfulness.

By going to a therapist and spending a lot of money, I managed to arrive at an acceptable diagnosis. I was unhappy and I needed treatment. A good psychoanalyst never gives you a prescription you can just fill, he won't tell you what to do and what not to do. Basically, he takes you by the hand and helps you to see yourself in the mirror. That's what a psychoanalyst's work consists of. It's up to you to take care of yourself and your desires. It's up to you to make your own decisions, it's up to you and no one else to make the necessary cuts and suffer accordingly.

True suffering is consummated in the fullness of solitude. The mouse that was inside of me wanted tranquility, serenity, happiness, and protection. And I was finally willing to listen to my inner tears and change my life. The bank had been my prison and I wanted to be a free woman, free as the wind. It's nice to know that the Roma are called the "sons of the wind." Well, I consider myself a daughter of the wind, and it doesn't matter a bit to me that I was adopted.

* * *

If there's one thing I remember well about Medina, it's the first time we started talking seriously.

"What kind of work do you do?" she asked me.

"I work for a bank."

"What do you do at the bank?"

"I manage the customers' savings."

"How do you persuade them to give you their money?"

"By making a rosy, positive prediction about the future," I replied.

"You promise good things."

"Exactly."

"And people believe you?"

"Yes."

"How do you do it?" she insisted.

"I know how to talk convincingly."

"Then you're doing *drabarimos*."

"Drabarimos? What's that?"

According to Roma tradition, *drabarimos* is palm reading. It's one of the few "trades" in the history of the Roma. In human life, work is fundamental. The profound crisis of the Roma people is due to the disappearance of a number of trades, such as caring for horses. The horse was at the center of economic and social life for many centuries. It was the means of transport par excellence. With the mass use of cars, horses vanished from the picture. That brought the Roma livelihood to its knees, and subsequently led to their isolation. Work is a powerful means of communication and socialization because it creates a network of contacts and connections. It's fundamentally a collective act. People always work together, never alone.

Another trade that is increasingly endangered is that of the carny. In the past, the Roma went from small town to small town, bringing amusements and games. Then that job was taken over by television. Now if you want to travel from one place to another you have to have permits and authorizations without end. The bureaucracy is pitiless with the Roma. And there are people who continue to call the Roma nomads. These days, all that's left is the word itself. It's a luxury that the Roma can no longer afford. Every country, every city, every township, every district, and every neighborhood insists on its own sacred territorial rights. It seems that expelling the Roma from one's personal domain has become every citizen's foremost duty. And why? They say that gypsies bring nothing but blight. I once heard with my own ears that damned Bellezza, or Bruttezza, at the Madama Cristina market talking about exterminating the gypsies of San Salvario. He said that they had turned Valentino Park into a rat's nest.

* * *

The world of money is filled with plenty of people who are completely crazy, truly sick individuals. I'm reminded of the surgeon Giulio Rossini, a client in his early seventies. He lived alone and had never married. He had a fortune in his bank account. He was never willing to invest. We did our best to talk him into it, but always in vain. There was a large bonus awaiting anyone who could succeed in hauling his money out into the river of the markets. Rossini wouldn't be budged. Never in my life have I seen anyone like him. His relationship with money was out of the ordinary. Every euro that left his account was a source of sorrow. Like the death of a family member.

"Do you know that I can smell money?" he told me one day with a broad smile.

"Don't people say that money has no odor?"

"They couldn't be more wrong."

"Then you have an exceptional gift," I added.

"I wouldn't call it a gift, I'd call it an infinite love."

"Love?"

"To me, money is like women."

"Really?"

That's right. He explained to me that he loved and had been

loved for many years now. What struck me was more the phrase "been loved" than the word "love." I can understand someone who is head over heels in love with money, but the idea of being loved in return by that money . . . It struck me as crazy. He did his all to persuade me.

"What is love?"

"It's a way of being happy," I replied.

"Exactly. And money gives me happiness."

"But what do *you* give to money?"

"Happiness."

"I don't understand."

"Being happy means having no fear of the future," he explained in a philosophical tone of voice.

"The future?"

It's true that Dr. Rossini is crazy or close to it, but he has a mental clarity that everyone envies. He has an extraordinary capacity to express complicated concepts, but in simple terms. When we're in love, we have no fear. We feel strong, not vulnerable. We swear oaths of undying love. The economists agree on one essential point, in spite of their disagreements on so many other topics: Capital is a coward. Why? Because money is afraid, money wants stability. Rossini considered himself a perfect lover, a paragon of fidelity.

"Love is also jealousy," he added with an attentive glance.

"True enough. But what does that have to do with money?"

"It has plenty to do with money, plenty."

"How so?"

"I've dedicated my life to money."

"Now I see."

In short, he's right. He's sacrificed his life for his money.

The world of finance is full of extravagant characters. It's hard to talk about them without bringing up Stefano Farini, one particularly unscrupulous broker. I can safely say that he's a genuine nutjob. "There's no difference between a broker and a gambler," he always used to tell me. There's the same addictive personality. The same damn force driving them to take one risk after another. They always go all in, put every last penny on the line. But in my view, there's a substantial difference. While a gambler puts his own funds at risk, the broker plays with other people's money. Isn't that unbelievable? Banking has nothing to do with science, with rational thought. It's all a game. A huge, cursed game. Money is a toy. Every so often the toy gets broken and the savers all cry over their misfortune. At that point they need a kiss on the forehead or a pat on the back, just like little children. Some phrases that could prove useful: "Nothing happened. We'll fix it all up. Come on, stop crying. Good boy."

Money makes people get sick. That's why a bank can become a hospital. You go there to save something. Sometimes they manage to work miracles, but other times they just make messes. I worked in the home mortgage sector. I noticed how one could go from a state of euphoria to one of total despair. I saw young couples taking out thirty-year mortgages. Sweet Jesus, thirty years. How do you manage to carry a cross on your shoulders for thirty years?

* * *

I don't remember how I came up with the idea of taking revenge on my former employer, the Savings Bank. I thought of something very simple. A small plan, easy to carry out, with no risks or complications. The managing director, the prime beneficiary of the whole situation, would be forced to reimburse the small savers that I helped to defraud. I decided to punish Counselor Barillo. He was the managing director of the Savings Bank during the years I worked there. I couldn't let him get away scot-free. The managers are these strange creatures of the banking system: They get million-dollar salaries and golden parachutes even when the bank is going under. Even if I'm not about to be able to change the system, I can still do my part to settle a few accounts.

I decided to put my plan into motion after the tragedy of Signora Giacometti. Poor woman! She lost all her savings on "toxic" assets. Her only real fault was that she trusted me blindly. Yes, I was the one who talked her into it. The little old lady did everything she could to get her money back, at least in part, but it was no good. The system has no pity. To her, the system, the bank, the branch office was a person, that is, me. There was no way to make her change her mind. In the end she found a way to make me pay. One night, she came to the apartment building where I lived and killed herself. She ate strychnine, which is a rat poison. The morning after, the doorman found her lifeless body. She'd left a note in which she explained the reasons for her suicide, placing the blame squarely on me.

From that day on, my life became a living hell. I was harassed by journalists and by other people's gazes. Once, at the local supermarket, I heard someone say as I went by: "That's the woman who murdered the little old lady." Try to tell them that I had nothing to do with it, or practically nothing. The truly guilty party is the system, the bank, and that gang of unscrupulous managers. All pointless. I decided to move into a different apartment, but the little old lady's ghost followed me everywhere. I stopped sleeping. At the bank, they suggested I might want to move to a new city, say Milan or Rome. But I couldn't accept that. I would die anywhere but Turin.

To get out of this situation I had no choice but to reimburse the small savers that I'd defrauded. In order to do that, I needed a new identity. I had to disappear, while staying in Turin. The ideal thing would have been to have some kind of a magic object, a ring or a hat, that could turn me invisible.

Unfortunately, that wasn't possible. I thought and thought, and I finally came up with a solution. I decided to turn to Medina, my Roma friend.

"I want to come live in your camp."

"You're joking, right?"

"No, I'm completely serious."

"Why?"

"I want to change my life. I'm not happy."

"You're crazy."

"Better to be crazy than unhappy."

It wasn't easy to talk Medina into it. I told her about my job, about Signora Giacometti. In other words, about my unhappy life. Obviously I made no reference to my plan for revenge. She understood that I was going through a period of crisis, and that all I needed was chance to change my surroundings and take a break. She wasn't especially convinced that the camp would be the ideal solution. Maybe it would be better to take a nice long trip somewhere foreign. Asia, for example, might be a good place to go.

We began to make our preparations. The most important factor in our success was good acting. I had to become a real gypsy woman. I decided to abandon my makeup, my look, my Italian identity. I bought an old trailer. Medina introduced me to her family at the camp, saying that I was an orphaned Rom who'd grown up in a *gadji* orphanage, and that I needed to stay with them for a while, after which I would leave. They welcomed me with open arms. An orphan always arouses compassion.

"This story has to remain secret," I impressed upon her more than once.

"Don't worry, I won't tell a soul."

"Perfect. Now all I need is a Roma name."

"There are plenty: Mavus, Mirsada, Rubinia, Jasmine."

"I like Drabarimos."

"That's not a name."

"It could be a nickname."

"Sure."

"It'll help me in my new profession: palm reading."

"All right. From now on I'll call you Drabarimos."

"I really like it."

If I have a gift, it's certainly for organization. I even got a master's in management. Putting together a plan that had to do with my life and involved only me was much simpler. After all, what's a plan? It's a route, an itinerary with clearly defined points of departure and arrival. The big problem is running without knowing where it is you're going.

On the day that Patrizia Pascali, namely me, shuffled off the stage, I arranged for my IDs and my purse to be found, along with a farewell note, by the banks of the Po. I remember it very clearly. I wrote a real tearjerker. This is how it began: "The moment has come to say farewell. I'm sorry it has to be this way. I don't want to go on living. I'd like to pull the plug and go away in silence. I ask you all to forgive me. Goodbye. Patrizia."

I went to live in my trailer in the camp by Valentino Park. A new life had started for me. A great adventure, whose ending remained open and unknown.

CHAPTER NINE
The gypsies are becoming civilized thanks to dogs

I slept briefly and poorly. That always happens to me when I'm stressed out. At home, I'm alone again. Tania went to Milan to see a girlfriend and she won't be back till tonight. My mother still hasn't come around. Could she be with Aunt Quiz, plotting against me? I wouldn't rule it out. Paranoia is an ugly thing. It makes you feel besieged. You try to run away, but it's an extremely difficult endeavor. To get rid of these nasty thoughts and do something useful, I decide to take long walk by the river Po. It's a good way to relax. I don't want to talk with anyone, or rather, there's only one person I want to talk to: Enzo Laganà. I'm having a meeting with myself. What's needed is a serious, heartfelt one-on-one. I'd like to analyze my professional standing, without filters and without fear. My personal and emotional life, praise the Lord, is going swimmingly, at least for the moment.

Where should we begin, then? Without a doubt, with the good little virgin of Via Ormea. Everything started with her damn lie. This affair brought me to a crossroads: Should I resign or keep my job as an asshole journalist who's treated worse than an ass? In these conditions, I can't go on. I'd like to take a break. Get the poisons out of my system. What poisons? The news, the media world, crime reporting, this shitty line of work. I feel like someone suffering from an ulcer who's gobbled down too much junk food. My mind is full of garbage. The time has come for me to throw it all up.

Why not think about changing professions? I'm still young,

and I have my whole life (well, within limits) ahead of me, as the saying goes. What else could I do? Right off the bat, let's rule out all jobs that would require a college degree. I don't have the slightest interest in going back to the university. The same goes for any kind of work that requires a uniform (soldier, fireman, cop, etc.). Serious discipline isn't the kind of thing yours truly is cut out for. Being a chef wouldn't be bad. I could give my creativity free rein. I have a few recipes up my sleeve, like Risotto alla Laganà, made with that fresh spicy Maghrebi sausage, *merguez*, and brown rice. I'd like to open my restaurant right here in San Salvario.

Lately, there are a lot more bars in this neighborhood. The locals are starting to complain. They have a hard time getting to sleep at night. They want to make their voices heard, convince the city government to issue fewer licenses. In the meantime rents keep going up, forcing artisans and small businessmen to move elsewhere. The danger is that in a few years we'll find ourselves with a neighborhood that's been completely transformed, an open-air club designed to make fans of the *movida* happy.

My mind wanders without any clear destination, but in the end it comes back to my first question: Should I quit right away or wait? And why go on waiting? Shouldn't my health be my first priority? Perhaps all I'm doing is running away like my friend Luciano says, a coward's move. Okay, I understand, but what do we want, a hero covered with medals and praise, but who lies cold in his grave? Is that what Enzo Laganà wants? No thank you. I don't like heroes and I don't like martyrs.

I need a strategy. The objective is to repair the damage. Salvini, Maritani, and the mass media are trying to cover up the news of the fake rape. They want to file the case away. Acquit the culprits. In short, get off scot-free without paying the price. They're trying to distract public opinion. But I'm not going along with it. I'm no longer willing to be the cooperative asshole.

The first step is to publish the good little virgin's confession.
Let it cost what it costs. Am I ready to give up my job or let my
employers make a show of firing me from the paper? You bet.
I'm extremely ready.

Maritani made a fool of me. He treated me like a child. I
have to be smarter than him, wilier, more of a goddamn son of
a bitch. Slamming the door behind you is easy and they'd be all
too happy to get rid of someone like me. There's not one person but a hundred, no, a thousand people who want to take my
place. There's an army of journalists wet behind the ears,
interns (cannon fodder, in short). The famous full-time job
continues to be an obsession for my young colleagues. They're
all after one. They're all desperately seeking jobs. With their
goddamn full-time job they can hurry down to the local bank
and get a mortgage. That's the first requirement banks ask for
when you're looking for a mortgage. The banks! Just saying
the word makes me anxious. If there's a job I'll never do in my
life, it's working in a bank. A world of rogues and thieves.
Though I guess I shouldn't generalize. They aren't all assholes.
There are exceptions, for instance, the former managing director of the Savings Bank, Guido Barillo, who recently decided
to give back the salary and retirement bonus he'd accepted.
This money will be used to establish a fund to pay back the
customers who lost their savings. A fine example, worth following. We need honest, respectable people like him to lead
our nation. I'd vote for someone like Barillo without giving it a
second thought.

Taking a short walk in blessed peace, admiring the waters
of the river Po, really helps me think. After a pleasant stroll,
here come the first fruits: A true son of a bitch of an idea starts
mosquitoing around in my ear.

I have to admit that my most diabolical ideas all include an
indispensable ingredient: prankish humor. And since we're in
the midst of a gypsy emergency, as my editor in chief puts it,

the term to use is *zingarata*—a gypsy prank, a nice collective practical joke. My most son-of-a-bitch ideas are born in my brain, but when it comes to actually putting them into action, a great many people take part, quite a few of them without realizing it. For that reason, I'm also a small-scale manipulator, though I do it for noble causes.

* * *

I call my friend Luciano Terni and ask him to meet me immediately about something extremely urgent. He tells me to rendezvous with him in a bar near Porta Palazzo, where he lives. A very nice part of town, with people who've come from all around the world. It doesn't take me long to get there. Luciano and I have known each other for many years. He has this amazing talent: He can imitate anyone's voice. He's an excellent theatrical actor. Usually I turn to him for little "artistic jobs." What are they? My secret weapons against bureaucracy. No one can take on a bureaucracy without plenty of patience. As my mother likes to say, I wasn't born with the gift of patience. And she's perfectly right. I have no hope of ever changing.

In order to move an application forward or get access to a confidential document, you need to file requests, you need permits, official stamps, embossed seals, authorizations. An intolerable torture for yours truly. Luckily, all it takes is a quick phone call to good old Luciano; I just ask him to imitate the voice of some official. But first I give him a recording of the person's voice, obtained illegally. And, perfectionist that he is, he gives it his all. The results have always been excellent. We've had many a laugh at the expense of unsuspecting victims.

Since the job is a delicate and risky one, we've adopted the same kinds of precautions employed in spying operations. We never speak to each other on the "official" telephone during the imitations, to avoid being found out. The safest way is to use a so-called ghost cell phone, a phone registered to a deceased person. We've never had any trouble. I have to admit that I was largely inspired by Alighiero Noschese when I came up with the prank. Noschese was an extraordinary impersonator, and his impressions of famous people—like Prime Minister Giulio Andreotti—were dead-on. It's said that once Andreotti's mother complained to her son that he'd neglected to let her know that he'd be appearing on a certain TV show. Actually it was Noschese who appeared, doing an imitation of Andreotti.

In 1979, Noschese was found dead; he'd committed suicide in mysterious circumstances at the Villa Stuart clinic in Rome, where he'd been admitted for severe depression. The official version stated that he'd shot himself with a pistol. Two years later, the list of the members of the P2 Masonic lodge was uncovered. And guess who was on it? None other than the great Alighiero Noschese. But what was someone like Noschese doing with the powerful men of the day? Perhaps the answer is contained in an interview with an anonymous general, given to *L'Espresso* in 1981: During the Years of Lead, when Italy was riven by terrorist violence, a very talented impressionist was used to derail investigations into state-sponsored massacres through a series of phone calls attributed to leading figures in the Italian government. An incredible story, worthy of a great thriller filled with plot twists.

Four years ago we undertook a series of memorable performances. In Turin, there had been a number of murders of Albanians and Romanians. The press had started talking about blood feuds, and even a third great Mafia war. The Albanians were the Palermitans, while the Romanians were the Corleone gang. What a lovely oversimplification. In any case, for that occasion we dreamed up three characters from the world of organized crime: the Albanian Buscetta, a boss who'd fallen

into disgrace, the Romanian Riina, a bloody *capo* who was trying to seize power, and Madame, a lady pimp who was running
a network of Nigerian prostitutes. The results were first-class;
we wound up on the front page more than once. One scoop
after another. Luckily, no one ever caught us. And as they say
in the soccer business: Don't mess with a winning team.
Luciano and I are a winning duo.

"I've found a way to get the good little virgin's confession
published," I tell him without beating around the bush.

"Have you managed to talk your bosses into it?"

"No. I don't think there's any way to persuade them," I
reply.

"What are you thinking?"

"About how to screw them."

"I like the idea, but how?"

"I need to make use of your gift."

"For an artistic job?"

"That's right."

"Do we have a script?"

"Certainly."

I explain my son-of-a-bitch idea to Luciano. It was that bastard Salvini who rejected my article about the good little virgin's confession. Maritani is nothing more than someone who
obeys orders. That's important in terms of figuring out where
to strike. There's no point in shooting at Maritani alias the Red
Cross. The question to ask is the following: What if Salvini
changed his mind and decided to publish it? All someone
would need to do is pick up the phone and call the managing
editor, Angelo Maritani, and it would be taken care of. It just
requires a little creativity and a little luck. That's all.

"Now I understand what you have in mind."

"Imitating Salvini's voice will be child's play," I insist.

"You know I like to prepare myself thoroughly."

"I know that."

"What exactly do I have to do?"

"Here's the script, my dear Luciano."

I'm very clear on the whole thing. Tonight Salvini (the fake one) is going to call the managing editor, Maritani, from an unknown number. He'll give the order to publish the confession. Maritani won't push back. Salvini is very authoritarian, he doesn't want to hear objections of any kind. The only thing he's happy to hear is compliments. Maritani won't dare to open his mouth; he's too disciplined, or rather, trained to obey orders.

"As you can see, it's a simple part," I say.

"There's no such thing as a simple part. I need to work on your editor in chief's voice."

"Don't worry about the material. You'll find a number of his most memorable performances on YouTube."

"And when are we going live?"

"Tonight."

"I don't like to be rushed," Luciano complains.

"I know that art and haste never go hand in hand, but unfortunately we don't have time."

First of all, we have to make sure that Maritani doesn't suspect a thing. We can't give him the time he'd need to check up on things, to call back Salvini, for example. The phone call should be made just before the newspaper goes to press, and yours truly will be present in person to make sure that the operation goes smoothly. You never know. Something could go sideways. At that point we'll have to promptly intervene and put Plan B into effect. The important thing is to be prepared for the worst. That's my philosophy of life. Is it a bit pessimistic? Sure. So what's wrong with that? A little healthy pessimism is only good for you. It helps keep you from losing touch with reality. In short, it's a form of elevated concentration. I've always said that minimizing the number of times you get screwed over ought to be an ideal objective to aim for every blessed day.

* * *

In the late afternoon Irene Morbidi gives me a call. We've known each other since elementary school. To her, animals are the only reason to live. She never stops waging battles on various fronts. Now she fights butchers, now the exclusion of dogs from public parks, now inhumane treatment of animals. Four years ago, she was one of the leading figures in the case of the piglet Gino. What a story that was! My friend and neighbor Joseph, a Nigerian and a Juventus fan, had adopted a piglet and had installed him on the balcony in front of his apartment. But good old Gino, a die-hard Juventus fan, had somehow wound up in the mosque on Via Galliari. Heaven forbid! There was quite a set-to between those who wanted to kill Gino outright, those who, like Bellezza, wanted to use him as a propaganda tool, and those who wanted to rescue him and adopt him, like Irene.

I catch up with her in the offices of her association in San Salvario.

"I'd like to ask for your help, Enzo."

"What can I do?"

"We want to bring the Roma back to their camp."

"Why?"

"It's a battle for civil rights."

"Why, what's become of you, Irene? Are you going to start defending the Roma now?"

"Actually, I'm more concerned about their fifteen dogs."

"What do the dogs have to do with anything?"

Irene will never change. For her, animals are the absolute priority. She explains to me that a few months ago the Roma in the camp adopted fifteen or so dogs to use in their panhandling operations. Irene and her partners in the association immediately mobilized to nip this new trend in the bud. Later they changed their minds: Dogs could actually help to improve the lives of the Roma and, especially, their image. How so? Dogs could put an end to that inhumane Roma tradition of using children to do their begging for them.

Irene never stops insisting on how useful dogs are in daily life, how they keep old people company, bring joy to children, help the blind, save human lives in the aftermath of an earthquake, catch drug traffickers in airports and train stations, and lots of other things. The list of benefits goes on and on.

Irene is very angry with the good little virgin of Via Ormea, who fucked with a wonderful experiment. The camp at Valentino Park was becoming a useful laboratory for developing highly original solutions to many problems that mankind has been struggling to solve for a long time. What can be done with the gypsies? It's a question that troubles governments and society at large.

"We've noticed that the dogs have managed to change the Roma," she explains.

"How do you mean?"

"They've become more humane, more civilized."

"Are you sure?"

"Certainly, it's all documented. Then there's another source of concern."

"What's that?"

"When the Roma were here, we could keep an eye on the dogs."

"But now you have no way of checking up on them."

"Exactly. Who knows, they might already be depressed," she adds.

"Depressed? Are you talking about the Roma?"

"No, the dogs. In civilized countries, they give animals anti-depressants."

"That's a new one."

"We're way behind, Enzo. Unfortunately, we're a third-world country."

"You're right about that."

"Plus, if they need money, they might sell the dogs to unscrupulous individuals," she adds.

"To the Chinese, for instance."

"I don't even want to think about it."

The relationship between the Roma and their dogs reminds me of a French movie from the mid-Seventies, *The Gypsy*. Alain Delon plays the role of a gypsy outlaw, a sort of latter-day Zorro. In a moment of rage, the gypsy, that is, Delon, says that dogs are treated better than gypsies and that a Roma woman is left to give birth in the garbage, to general indifference.

Irene asks me to lend her a hand with the media, using my position as a journalist. What can I do? It's simple. At least in theory. We need to persuade the citizens of San Salvario to let the Roma and their dogs—especially their dogs—return, for the good of the community, no, of humanity. In San Salvario, we're working to solve once and for all the gypsy emergency. The world is watching.

I promise to do what I can for this exceedingly noble humanitarian and pro-dog cause. I leave feeling disproportionately moved. I'm touched and I'm happy. I want to break into tears, but I can't quite do it. "Give me a tear so I can cry," goes an old song. The gypsies are becoming civilized thanks to dogs. There's a magnificent revolution! Why did it ever take us so long to understand?

* * *

I spend the evening in the newsroom instead of going to the Porta Nuova train station to meet my girlfriend and take her out to dinner.

At 11 P.M. I go over to Maritani's office. I knock and then go in. My managing editor isn't much of an actor; I can read everything on his face. He turns a fake fucking expression in

my direction; it drips hypocrisy. He's a huge son of a bitch.
Screwing him over is my moral duty.

"I'm sorry about that whole thing with the article, Enzo."

"Don't worry about it, Angelo."

"I tried with Salvini but he wouldn't listen to me."

"Still, I have to thank you for making the effort," I add.

"Unfortunately, I'm not the commander of the vessel," he
insists in a disconsolate tone.

"I know that, Angelo."

"Enzo, can I say something to you, as a friend?"

"Sure."

"No one resigns just because an article wasn't published."

"You're right. I lost my temper."

Maritani is acting the part of a school principal. Obviously
he sees me as a middle-school student. He indulges in a mono-
logue filled with advice and recommendations on the journalist's profession. He recounts a couple of anecdotes about
things that happened to him during his career. The first has to
do with an investigation into corruption in the Milan city government, a story he worked on for a whole month. In the end,
they simply tossed it. Why? Because it might have displeased
the majority party in the coalition government. Bad publicity
can be damaging, especially during an election. The second, on
the other hand, has to do with the big lesson of the Watergate
case, which forced the American president Richard Nixon to
resign: confidence, that's right, confidence. If Ben Bradlee, the
editor in chief of the *Washington Post*, hadn't had confidence
in his two young journalists, Woodward and Bernstein, we
would never have had the legendary journalistic coup, recognized the world over, that was Watergate. The message is loud
and clear: I have to trust him and his fucking editor in chief. I
feel like telling him to go to hell, right then and there. But I
decide not to snap back or contradict him. What good would
it do? None.

Watergate! Again with this fucking legend. An associate FBI director wants to get some revenge on the White House, and we wind up with this journalistic legend. Maritani likes legends, but I don't. We're very different people; there's a yawning gap between our two personalities. I let him talk without opening my mouth. Luckily, Maritani is forced to interrupt his homily so he can answer his cell phone. I was starting to get a little fed up. I hope it's Salvini calling—the fake one, of course.

"Yes sir, Mr. Editor in Chief . . . I'm sitting her with Enzo Laganà right now . . . Okay, I'll put this on speakerphone."

"Hi, Laganà. I reread your article, it's a great piece."

"Thanks, Mr. Editor in Chief," I reply.

"I think we're making a mistake by not publishing it. Do you hear what I'm saying, Maritani?"

"Yesterday you said not to publish it . . ." Maritani replies.

"Yesterday is yesterday, today is today, do you follow me, Maritani?"

"Certainly, Mr. Editor in Chief."

"Well, now I'm telling you to publish it."

"In its entirety, Mr. Editor in Chief?" Maritani asks.

"Yes, without changing so much as a comma," Salvini insists.

"But when?"

"In tomorrow's edition."

"We might not be in time, Mr. Editor in Chief."

"I'm giving you carte blanche to do what you need to do. I'm out and I left my cell phone at home. I'm calling from a friend's phone. But I want you to do whatever it takes, Maritani."

"Understood, Mr. Editor in Chief. I'm on it."

The phone call went very well. Luciano was magnificent as always. He sounded like Salvini in person. The voice was identical. Everything went smooth as silk, as per the script. Maritani asks me if I would be so kind as to send him the article by email immediately. If the article actually gets published, it's going to be nothing but trouble for Maritani. Salvini will dance on his grave. In the meantime, he's been authorized by the editor in chief (the fake one) himself to call the central newsroom and have them rush the good little virgin's confession into print.

I'll have to wait until tomorrow morning to see if the plan turns out successfully. You never know. It's better to be cautious. In any case, I go home feeling a little more relaxed after all these stressful days. I can't wait to turn my back on this story. Tania is already sleeping. I don't want to wake her up. I slip into bed and wrap my arms around her. She wakes up. Our bodies search and . . . find each other.

The first time I went around dressed as a gypsy woman, I felt very strange indeed. I truly was another person. I was struck by the way other people looked at me. I'd decided not to ask for charity, at least at first. I wanted to take things nice and slow. I wanted to try to use my knowledge of palm reading. Perfect my profession as a *drabarimos*, so that I'd truly deserve my nickname. I had some aces up my sleeve. I knew Italians only too well; I knew their strengths and weaknesses. All I needed to do was put my know-how into play.

I began over by the university. My first targets were the students. A world that I know very well. I chose exam time. We're all a little superstitious. Personally, I would just as soon not come across a black cat on the highway. Before finals, students are in need of reassurance. My job was to offer a little psychological support. And in return I certainly had a right to fair compensation.

I remember my first "client." She was a very attractive student. She was sitting alone, studying a statistics textbook. I went over, making sure I wasn't bothering her. She thought I was about to ask her for money. The wrong approach. In marketing, the first rule is: earn your customer's trust.

"Are you ready?" I asked her with a smile.

"It's going to be tough exam," she replied.

"It'll go fine. I can see it," I told her with great assurance.

"How?"

"Show me your hand."

I took her hand lightly and looked her in the eye. I stared down at her palm and pretended I was concentrating. I tried to detach myself from the real world and establish a privileged line of communication with the world of mysteries. I remained silent for more than a minute. Her curiosity grew. At a certain point, I started muttering to myself in a very low voice. It was as if I were addressing someone invisible.

"What is it?" she asked me, now quite curious.

"I can see you leaping from a very high place."

"Am I falling?" she asked, a little worried.

"No."

"Where am I?"

"In the mountains," I replied, continuing to hold her hand and look at her.

"I love the mountains."

"And in fact you look very happy to me."

There was no need to add any other details. The interpretation goes without saying. What is an exam, after all? It's leaping over an obstacle. The mountains are a familiar place. So why be afraid? The student was very pleased with my performance, with the services rendered. She felt reassured. She could walk into the exam with confidence. Before saying goodbye, she slipped a ten-euro note into my pocket.

That day something I already knew was confirmed: Human beings are very fragile, they constantly need to be reassured. Certainly, compared with our ancestors who were afraid of everything—snow, wind, disease, the sea, volcanoes—today we've learned to control many of our fears. With others, however—earthquakes, certain types of cancer, to say nothing of death itself—it's impossible.

There's not a newspaper or magazine that doesn't include a horoscope. Isn't that another form of *drabarimos*? In the office we'd comment on them every day. Actually, it's all a process of projection. We are trying to calm our fears, our terrors, our anxieties. We want promises of happiness: We're about to meet the great love of our lives, or we're about to come into a great deal of money. We like to be given certain kinds of warnings: don't put your trust in false friends, don't overdo it with food, don't miss out on great opportunities. It's the easiest thing to connect predictions to your own daily life. And that's the game right there. It's incredible the way people fall for it, hook, line, and sinker.

All the same, there are some incredible stories about telling the future. The story involving the foreign correspondent Tiziano Terzani is the craziest of them all. He tells that story in his fine book, *A Fortune-Teller Told Me.* In 1976 Terzani was a correspondent in Asia. One day, an old Chinese fortune-teller in Hong Kong warned him: "Beware! In 1993 you'll run the risk of being killed. Don't take a plane that year. Never fly anywhere." Terzani took the prophecy seriously. He decided not to fly at all that year, going everywhere on foot, or by car, train, or ship. A laborious approach, but one that allowed him to discover the depths of Asia and its poorest citizens, their everyday stories, their great hopes. It was an adventure full of surprises and opportunities. During that year, one of Terzani's colleagues died in a plane crash—while he was filling in for Terzani on a business trip. The prophecy had come true. It's hard to find an explanation. That's just how it is.

I myself was the subject of a prophecy. Granny Mavus, a genuine gypsy woman who spent a few days in the camp before going on to join her children in France, told me: "My daughter, you will die soon. Your death will be a brief winter, without cold, without rain, but with heat and fire."

Actually, my work at the bank wasn't much different from that of the gypsy woman who does *drabarimos* or Terzani's fortune-teller. I did this same kind of work with my savers. I told them how to proceed in the uncertain and complicated world of finance. Invest in the safest products and avoid risks.

I couldn't do my job without becoming involved in the predictions game.

One time I read a very interesting article. In Canada and the United States there are men of Roma descent who practice *drabarimos* in the field of finance. They serve as consultants to stock market investors, suggesting how and when to buy and sell stocks. It used to be that only women read palms, but now there are also men who read not palms, but stock portfolios. In other words, the paths of *drabarimos* really are infinite. The watchword wherever you turn is always the same: make money. And to do that, you have to be able to read the future.

In spite of technology, development, and modernity, human beings are fragile. They continue to be afraid of the forces of nature. They try to keep everything under control, but that's impossible. Still, many persist, with a certain amount of arrogance. They make me laugh when they talk about market trends, the stock exchange. How can you mix up the stock market with the changes in the weather? You can get it right every so often, but you'll never get it right every time.

One of the founding fathers of capitalism, Adam Smith, spoke of an invisible hand, a mysterious force that drives the individual to pursue his selfish goals. At the same time, without really wanting to, he benefits the society he lives in. I like this invisible hand, outside of anyone's control. There are still those who maintain that the crux of democracy is transparency. But how can we have both the invisible hand and transparency, both the blessed invisible hand and democracy, both the cursed invisible hand and the rules of the market?

* * *

I spent my first few months in the camp just observing. I wanted to figure out how things worked. Of course I asked lots of questions, especially of Medina. I immediately realized that there are rules that must be followed. An unwritten code of conduct. The hierarchy is fundamental. Women play an important role, but they don't have as much power as men. Exactly the same as in Italian society. Just take a look at the membership of the Italian parliament. Female representation is minimal, little more than symbolic. Children are raised in a very particular way. There's a determination to turn them into adults as quickly as possible. It's the law of survival. Before becoming a gypsy woman, I had a negative impression of the Roma mother, a heartless woman who uses her children ruthlessly. I was convinced that Roma women didn't love their children, but it turns out that's not true at all. A mother is still a mother.

All the same, their educational system is very different from ours. For the Roma, the transition to adulthood takes place quite quickly. The little ones are expected to take care of themselves and rely on their own resources.

Once I talked with Medina about the widespread fear that the Roma steal children. She started laughing and there was no way to get her to stop.

"Drabarimos, we don't steal children, it's the other way around."

"What do you mean?"

"Social services."

"And what is it they do?"

"They steal our children."

"How?"

Medina explains to me that the Roma, the women especially, are tremendously afraid of social workers. When an underage Roma is arrested, for theft, say, the responsibility falls on his parents. The charge is that they're incapable of adequately caring for their child, so he must be handed over to social services.

At the camp I noticed three women who carried their babies in their arms when they went out to beg. Something that always disgusted me. You can't use little children like that. It's bad for their health. I told myself: "We need to find not an alterative to charity, but an alternative to the use of little kids." Little by little, this became a problem for me. I was trying to find a solution. I had a profound desire to help these people to improve their living conditions. One day I had an idea. I immediately discussed it with Medina.

"Asking for charity with a child in your arms is frowned upon," I started things by saying.

"I know. Unfortunately there's no other solution," she replied, throwing her arms in the air.

"There are always alternatives. You just have to seek them out."

"A child inspires tenderness."

"You're wrong there, Medina."

I explain to her with brutal frankness that people couldn't care less about the Roma and their children. Forget about tenderness! Many Italians see it quite differently. And with their comments, they exclude the Roma from the human race. That's why they use words like extermination, cleansing, rat's nest. The language is never innocent. Behind every act there exists a word.

"What are you thinking?" Medina asked me.

"I think I know how we can replace the children."

"With who?"

"With dogs."

"Are you joking?"

"No," I said, looking at her seriously.

Medina's reaction wasn't long in coming: She burst out laughing like a crazy person. And, as is always the case, her laughter proved contagious. I started laughing with her. I explained the idea to her, based on my own experience. When I chanced to see a gypsy woman with a child in her arms asking for money, I was annoyed, it was repugnant to me. Of course it never even occurred to me to give her a coin. It was impossible for me to feel an ounce of compassion. The wall of rejection was insurmountable. One sure thing is that we Italians don't like seeing children used as bait. But we love dogs, and we spend quite a bit of money on their care. Just go to any supermarket and take a look at the aisles set aside for pet products, to say nothing of actual pet stores. In brief, we treat them like human beings. Medina listened to me carefully. In the end, she came around.

She was full of enthusiasm and didn't want to waste any time. We set right to work, trying to find an ideal candidate willing to lend itself to our noble cause. After a few days, we found a little abandoned dog. We took care of him and named him Oscar II. For fifteen years I'd had a little dog whose name was, in fact, Oscar. I really loved that dog. When he died, I was unable to get another. The void he left in my life was impossible to fill.

After a few days, Oscar II had recovered. I immediately realized that he was a very intelligent dog, in addition to being handsome and likable. My intuition was sound. Before long, he'd become the camp's mascot. The children had fun playing with him.

Before beginning our experiment, I gave Medina a few lessons on how to behave. I taught her how to pick up and hold Oscar II, for example, how to pet him, and lots of other tricks. The first few times I went with her, we sat down outside a supermarket. The results were outstanding. People didn't look at us, they looked at Oscar II. They asked us his name and how old he was. They petted him. Many of them were deeply moved when they discovered that Oscar II was a foundling and that we'd rescued him from the streets. Gypsies as the saviors of abandoned dogs. Unthinkable. We got lots of donations. One lady who had a dog wanted to semi-adopt Oscar II, offering to bring food for him on a regular basis. Another one offered to pay his vet bills. It couldn't have gone any better.

Oscar II brought a great change. The women were on board. We decided to scale up. We went looking for other abandoned dogs. No one trusted the gypsies enough to give them their puppies. After a lot of looking, we managed to find five beautiful dogs. Medina and I took care of teaching the women. Everything went fine and we didn't have to wait long for results. Instead of walking the whole time with a child in your arms and enduring an endless stream of insults, all we had to do now was simply choose a place, a post office or a super-market, and sit down. And people would come to us. Conver-sation ensued and the donations abounded.

After two weeks, though, a problem developed. An Italian woman who lives in San Salvario started bothering us. She claimed that we were mistreating our animals, that we were exploiting them pitilessly.

So I decided to intervene right away to forestall further complications. I went with Medina to the Madama Cristina market. We sat down next to a supermarket entrance. Oscar II was with us, handsomer than ever. At a certain point, we saw a tall, skinny woman come over. Medina gestured to let me know this was her. Before saying a word, the woman petted Oscar II, whispering a few words to him. She seemed like someone who knew how to talk to animals.

"What you're doing is a horrible thing," she said in an angry voice.

"What harm are we doing?" I replied quite calmly.

"You're using dogs to beg!"

"We don't force anyone to give us anything," Medina retorted.

"It's unacceptable to exploit defenseless animals like this."

"We aren't doing anything wrong. We love our dogs," I insisted.

"Come on, a dog isn't a toy. A dog requires attention and care. This new trend will have grave consequences," she added.

"All we're trying to do is make ends meet," Medina replied.

"You aren't even capable of taking care of yourselves," the woman added, piling on.

"Are you saying that we're inferior? How dare you? You're a racist!" I shouted right in her face.

"That's not what I said."

The woman defended herself, saying that everyone in San Salvario knew about the work she'd done on behalf of immigrants. Her battle had always been the same: to defend the rights of the weakest. And in this case the dogs are more vulnerable than the Roma.

I realized that this woman was a decent person. At that point I tried to establish a line of communication. I explained to her that we don't mistreat our dogs. That we'd rescued them from the street. Then, to impress her, I pulled out a health certificate from the vet. Obviously quite impressed, she sat down beside us and picked up Oscar II. She started kissing him and playing with him. At that point she looked at me and asked:

"What's the name?"

"I'm Drabarimos."

"No, the dog's name."

"Oscar II."

"Beautiful name. And what are you called again?"

"Drabarimos, and this is my friend Medina."

"My name is Irene Morbidi. I'm the president of the PARA association—'Proud Animal Rights Activists.'"

"Nice to meet you."

"Why do you speak such good Italian, Drabarimos?"

"I was born and raised in Turin," I replied.

From that day forth, Irene stopped bothering us. Though she never stopped checking in to make sure we were taking care of the dogs. We invited her to come to the camp several times to see how they were faring. She was truly surprised.

I wake up late. Tania went to a museum downtown. The idea of going to museums is something I've never understood. Standing around in an enclosed space with lots of other people and staring at canvases or statuettes doesn't strike me as very fun. I don't want to be taken for the kind of guy who hates museums, but I do think it's more useful to focus on the present and the future. And after all, it takes a great deal of imagination to find a way into a work of art. To say nothing of meditation. That's right, meditation: a way of concentrating by detaching yourself from the present, from reality, from the world that surrounds us.

Tania's never forced me to go to a museum with her. For my part, I've returned the favor. To her, soccer is a stupid sport, the most idiotic invention in human history: "Twenty-three people, including both goalies and the referee, chasing after a ball," she says to me over and over. I've never asked her to watch a Juventus match on TV or to come with me to the stadium. That would be genuine torture for her, especially because of the shouting of the fans. Tania likes silence. She's always done yoga and she's practiced many different forms of meditation. So we made a pact: We never go to museums or soccer matches together.

* * *

It's all just a matter of luck. Viagra was discovered accidentally.

Researchers working for Bayer were trying to come up with a pharmaceutical to combat hypertension. The medicine was administered to a group of patients. But the experiment yielded an unexpected result: The patients' blood pressure didn't diminish, but the volunteers of the male sex did get erections. Aunt Quiz always warns wives of a certain age to beware of husbands who turn into stallions in heat. Giacomo the bartender breaks in to say that Viagra is just sexual doping. A man who uses it to put on an impressive performance is a fraud. Then he vents his envy: "Our soccer is completely fake; there are teams, like Juventus, that use doping to win the championship." I decide not to reply. Giacomo is a Torino F.C. fan, and his team hasn't won a thing in years. Last season they spent plenty of time in Serie B. So what do they still want from us? They tossed us out of Serie A back in 2006 thanks to Calciopoli, the game-fixing scandal, but we came back bigger and better than ever.

In spite of the anti-Juventus atmosphere, Giacomo's café holds a great many memories for me, especially from my child-hood. When I was little, I went there with my father on week-ends. The café was a sort of second living room; we'd meet friends and people from back home. People would play cards and talk (and talk) and smoke (and smoke and smoke) and joke around, swap lots of information.

I never got bored there. I was fascinated, and for a few hours I entered into the world of adults. I liked that masculine atmosphere. And the thing I liked best was being treated like a man, a little man. Everyone shook my hand, my father's relatives and friends added a couple of kisses. I was shown the utmost respect. In this café I was no longer a child, I was something a little more—though I can't say that I was a fully formed man, either. I wasn't, for example, allowed to smoke a cigarette, or order a coffee or a beer. But that didn't bother me in the slight-est. I wasn't complaining, I was happy with a Coca-Cola.

As I enjoy my breakfast in blessed peace, I reach out my hand and grab the paper. Here's some good news: Our plan to screw Salvini and Maritani has worked perfectly. Luciano has scored yet another goal with his umpteenth masterful performance. My scoop on the good little virgin has wound up on the front page. Hooray! There's a banner headline: THE GIRL WHO FAKED A RAPE SPEAKS. Underneath, there's my byline. I've never been as happy about a front-page story as I am about this one. Let's just say that I sweated this one more than I did the others. But there's no sign of Editor in Chief Salvini's editorial. He didn't have the time to churn out his usual bullshit. What I wouldn't give to be able to see him when his eyes land on the front page. I can just imagine his reaction. Will he have a heart attack?

I check the content; nothing has been changed. Those assholes didn't have the necessary time. What a pleasant, if small, moral victory. I consider myself quite satisfied, but only in part. I still can't say that justice has been done. The harm suffered by the Roma in general and by the Roma at the camp in Valentino Park in particular is incalculable. They were forced to flee in haste and panic like so many chicken thieves. I don't know what can be done to pay them back. But it's going to take a little something extra. In the meantime, we can settle up the first installment on our debt with the good little virgin's confession; then we'll get busy settling up the rest. Personally, I hate being in any kind of debt. If there's one thing I'm proud of, it's that I've never been ripped off by a bank. I've never invested in a goddamn stock in my life. They've tried everything they could think of (even enlisting my mamma) to talk me into taking out a mortgage on an apartment, but I've always refused. I'm stubborn, a real diehard. I turned a deaf ear to their siren songs: "Renting is like dumping your money into the sea," "Enzo, wake up, make your savings bear fruit," "Bricks and mortar are the only sure thing," "Never stop investing, make sure your capital grows," "Money parked in a bank is like abandoned farmland," "Don't be a fool," "Take advantage of the bargains while they're still around," and blah blah blah.

Almost two years ago, Aunt Quiz went through a really bad period; she was going crazy with sorrow and worry. She'd invested a substantial portion of her savings in stocks. It was those bastards at the bank, where she'd been a client practically all her life, who talked her into it. And she trusted them. Luckily it went better for her than it did for Signora Giacometti, God rest her soul. I personally reported on that heartbreaking story and I remember all the details very clearly. Signora Giacometti, eighty-two, committed suicide in front of the apartment of the woman who ran the branch office where she'd invested her life savings. A long life, full of sacrifices and economies. One day she came to the newspaper in tears, asking for help. I still remember the day. She wanted to fight the branch office, but she was all alone. Maritani promised we'd do something about it, that we'd cover her case, but those were only words. Why didn't he keep his promise? Because the last thing he wanted to do was attack the banking system. The little old lady had a dispute with the same bank that's still one of our newspaper's biggest advertisers.

Signora Giacometti did everything she could to get her money back, but in the end she realized that David can't defeat Goliath. At least not always. People advised her over and over to sue the bank. A battle that was lost before it began. The poor woman didn't have a penny left to her name, how could she pay a lawyer? In the end, she decided to take revenge on the bitch from the branch office who had defrauded her, and right outside her apartment building. And then the woman from the bank, in turn, killed herself, too, by throwing herself into the river Po. Her corpse was never found.

My cell phone rings. It's that asshole Maritani.

"Things are a mess here, Enzo."

"What's happened?"

"Salvini is beside himself."

"Because he wasn't invited to appear on *Rear Window*?"

I'd like to have a little fun. One of a fan's greatest joys is mocking an opposing team's fan. As a Juventus partisan I have quite the repertoire. I'm very good at winding people up. My victims are, for the most part, supporters of A.C. Milan, Inter Milan, and, especially, Torino F.C. Of course, I know the reason for the mess. Salvini is angry at Maritani for having published the good little virgin's confession without his express permission. His authority as editor in chief has been called into question. What the fuck is he doing behind that goddamned desk if there's a managing editor of a local edition making decisions in his place, eh? You have to put yourself in his shoes. Doesn't the editorial hierarchy mean anything these days? Are we heading for pure anarchy? What's going to become of the newspaper?

Poor Maritani swears he obeyed Salvini's orders. He would never get it into his head to do a thing on his own. He's always preferred the role of the well-disciplined soldier. Now, in order to clear matters up, he needs an eyewitness who can also serve as a judge. My testimony can make all the difference. I was the only person present during the phone call in question. I pretend to have no idea what he's talking about. My managing editor is trembling with fear. He doesn't know which way to turn. He's not accustomed to conflict. He really might be about to lose his job.

"I don't understand a thing, Enzo."

"Neither do I, Angelo."

"Salvini denies ever calling. Can you believe it?"

"Inconceivable!" I agree.

"I made a terrible mistake by not recording the call."

"Now what's going to happen?" I ask.

"All he said was that there are going to be consequences."

"You'll see, it'll all turn out fine."

"I need to ask you a favor, Enzo. Call Salvini."

"I don't think that's a very good idea, Angelo."

"Why not?"

"He'll just dig his heels in even more."

And here come the myriad pains in the ass, right on time. I don't like favors. Why not? When you do someone a favor, the exact same thing always happens: you pull him out of the shit, which is a fine and noble thing, but, at the same time, you put yourself in *his* situation. It's very simple: The check always has to be paid. Now, I have no intention of rescuing Maritani and sacrificing poor Enzo Laganà. I'll do whatever it takes to keep from falling into the trap by stalling for time. And yours truly is a real master at that particular game. In any case, Maritani comes around to my way of thinking. Having me call Salvini to defend his innocence might prove counterproductive. Our editor in chief is both touchy and stubborn. He'll think we're plotting against him in order to steal his job. In short, he'll feel like the victim of a full-fledged coup. Better to let him think that this was an isolated event, an involuntary error on the part of one of his managing editors.

As for me, I hope it all goes to hell. The two of them are assholes and sons of bitches! To hell with them. I feel no compassion. What's happening is the very least that they could have expected. Bastards! The show has just begun. I'm willing to swear that it will all be very entertaining.

* * *

When lunchtime rolls around Luciano calls me and asks if I want to go the hospital with him to pay a visit on Drabarimos: That's the name of the injured Roma woman. We arrange to meet at the front entrance of Molinette Hospital. Luciano is very relieved, the injured child is out of danger. We take advantage of the opportunity to talk about my new piece.

"Nice scoop, Enzo."

"Thanks to your excellent performance."

"It wasn't hard to imitate that little piece of shit Salvini."

"There's plenty of material in his television appearances," I add.

"Do you know that I'm thinking about putting together a play based on this story?"

"Nice idea. Have you already decided on a title?"

"Yes. *The Virgin of Via Ormea.* What do you think?"

"You can do better."

"Let's hear from the master of headlines."

"*The Splendid Prank of the Good Little Virgin of Via Ormea.*"

"Not bad. Why don't we write it together?"

"Good idea. I'll start a new career in theater and close the door on my life as a journalist."

We get to Drabarimos's hospital room. The door is open. She greets us with a smile. Her hands are still bandaged. Luciano looks at her in a very specific way. My sixth sense tells me that there's something going on between the two of them. Luciano hasn't told me anything. I'll force him to confess, though, one way or another. A romance with a gypsy would be a major step forward in terms of reconciling himself with his roots.

"Thanks for the article," Drabarimos tells me.

"It's just a small attempt at reparation," I reply in a voice full of modesty.

Luciano won't let me get away with the word "reparation." How can anyone make reparations to the Roma people for centuries of oppression? It's impossible. The world has yet to acknowledge the *Porajmos*, the Romani holocaust, the half-million people who died in the Nazi death camps. Still, today, as in the story of the good little virgin, gypsies remain perfect scapegoats.

Drabarimos is more optimistic than either of us. She believes that what happened at San Salvario will serve as a warning for the future. I'm not especially convinced. There've been so many lessons in the recent past. So many people have shouted: "Never again!" And, after a while, we all go back to making the same mistakes, sometimes even worse than before. The problem is that our sense of guilt never seems to last long.

I stay with them for another ten minutes or so, then I decide it's time to leave. I have bad memories of hospitals from when my father was sick. Drabarimos made an excellent impression on me. I think she's a very sharp woman.

* * *

In the late afternoon, I go to the newsroom. They tell me that Maritani is out. He's probably been summoned to appear before Salvini, the paper's supreme judge. I don't know if there's going to be a disciplinary hearing. The one thing I do know is that Salvini is the vindictive type. This time, Maritani really could lose his job. I don't know how he's going to manage this one. Maybe he has some guardian angel who'll look out for him.

While I'm surfing the Internet I see Silvana, the clever intern, come in. She wants to talk to me, but she gets off on the wrong foot.

"If you address me as 'sir' one more time I'll make sure they fire you. Is that clear?"

"Understood, Enzo."

"That's much better. Go ahead, I'm listening."

"I wanted to talk to you about some reporting I'm doing on underage call girls here in Turin."

"How can I help?"

"Apparently Virginia, the Virgin of Via Ormea, was caught up in the circuit."

"First of all, do me a favor. Don't call her the virgin anymore, call her the good little virgin. Understood?"

Silvana shows me her work. There are file folders full of information. She spent a couple of months interviewing young girls, parents, teachers. It's a widespread phenomenon, not only in Turin but all over Italy. Young girls who sell their bodies, especially online, to earn money and to satisfy various needs: It's how they get designer clothing and piercings, how they're able to show off the latest iPhone. Some of them venture beyond the realm of the virtual. They arrange meetings with men who are willing to pay a lot for an hour of company. The most troubling thing has to do with the parents. They're completely unaware. We live in a consumer society where everything is for sale, and everything can be bought.

"Exactly what do you know about our good little virgin?"

"One source assured me that she was involved in the trade," she replies.

"Who's your source?"

"I'm sorry. I can't reveal that."

"Good work, Silvana."

I told you the young woman was wide-awake. I wasn't wrong. She's going to go far. Sources are sacred in our profession. You've got to do everything you can to maintain professional confidentiality. Silvana is using the source as bait to get me to take the hook. If I agree to work with her on this project, she'll reveal her source. I thank her for thinking of me, but I explain that yours truly prefers to work alone. In the end, I promise to help her and assure her that she can turn to me for suggestions and advice. This young woman reminds me of my own early days. Lots of enthusiasm, and plenty of passion. She'll forge her own path and make her own discoveries. That's the way life is. No one can live anyone else's life and, in the end, it's just like that wise Maghrebi proverb says: "Every man goes into the grave alone."

* * *

I spend the evening at home. Blessed among four women: Aunt Quiz, Natalia, Tania, and, of course, my mother. Mamma's made a fine dinner. I'm increasingly struck by how well my mother and Tania get along. By now, we can safely say they're colluding. I just hope that she hasn't been recruited as a spy. Anything's possible. My mother is a remarkably gifted seducer and persuader. Aunt Quiz never tires of pointing out how famously the two women get along. Apparently, Tania has passed all the tests. She's even been invited to come visit Calabria sometime in the next few months. Probably so the consultations can continue. Now Aunt Quiz breaks the ice.

"How many years have you been together?" she asks us.

"Almost six years," Tania replies.

"Then what are you waiting for?" she adds, turning to me.

"I don't understand, Auntie," I reply.

"Don't pretend you don't get it, Enzo."

"But I don't," I insist.

"Marriage," Natalia says tersely.

As far this subject goes, my mother limits herself to merely observing. She doesn't have much to say. Actually, she has no reason to speak. She has two first-class spokespeople. Aunt Quiz and Natalia are more than enough for her purposes.

We spend a pleasant evening together. It's been a long time since I've seen my mother like this, happy and full of joy. Every so often she looks at me, her gaze filled with tenderness and love. I'm almost touched.

CHAPTER TWELVE
Every system has a flaw

A fter a few months living in the camp, I became a gypsy. Physically, I really was unrecognizable. Patrizia Pascali had vanished. Drabarimos had taken her place. The truth is that without makeup I'm another person, and that without my designer clothes no one who knew me would for a moment think that behind the gypsy woman there could possibly be Patrizia the bank employee. So I was invisible. And I was very pleased with the outcome. A professional actress couldn't have done any better.

I had wanted to earn the nickname "Drabarimos," and now I finally had. I enjoyed reading palms and predicting the future, using all the information I had on my compatriots. At that point, I decided to get business cards to more easily spread the word. Actually, I didn't need an office, it was enough to have a cell phone so I could take calls from my customers. After a couple of months, I was able to land five steady clients, four women and a man. Often I met them at Valentino Park, just a stone's throw from the camp. My work was very simple: I had to listen to them and then reassure them.

One day I wanted to feel even more like a gypsy, push my identity to an extreme. I wanted to go on reading palms but I also wanted to diversify, professionally. It's a good idea to diversify your products and investments, not only in business and the world of banks and finance, but also in everyday life. So I decided to panhandle. At first it wasn't easy; I was extremely ashamed. Then I screwed up my courage and I plunged into it. I have a weakness for adventures. The first few times, I was overwhelmed by the insults. But the offensive words weren't what hurt me most; it was the glances filled with silence. I don't think that there's anything crueler than indifference. It's the ultimate insult.

After a series of attempts during which I didn't collect much, in fact not much at all, I changed my tactics. My years at the bank had to be good for something. I've always managed to convince people to give me their money. I had some very good cards to play. So it occurred to me to read from a script that had produced unbelievable results. I'd go over to the candidate, male or female, and start in on my routine.

"Pardon the disturbance." That's how I began my pursuit.

"Go away!"

"Signora, please don't treat me badly."

"What do you want?"

"I'm not the gypsy that I seem. I'm Italian, 100 percent Italian, just like you."

"I told you to go away."

"What happened to me could happen to you. The wheel of life never stops turning."

"What do you want from me?"

"Please help me, I'm begging you," I add in a despairing voice.

If the candidate, male or female, shows even the slightest interest in me and is willing to go on listening, then my work is done. I tell them that I once had a family, a home, and a job. I was happy and content. Then everything went wrong. Unfortunately I lost everything in the recession and I found myself penniless, living on the street. I didn't need to weep. That tragic story was more than enough.

Often, I found I provoked a feeling of solidarity. Why? Because the same thing could happen to them. They're terrified that they might find themselves in my shoes. This experience taught me that perhaps the hatred Italians feel toward gypsies actually springs from their fear of winding up like them one day, from their fear of being rejected, insulted by everyone, treated like vermin. You need only become poor to be seen as no different from gypsies.

* * *

During my stay at the camp by Valentino Park I never lost sight of my principal mission: to do whatever I could to secure reimbursements for the poor clients I did so much to defraud. I had a list of the clients I'd cheated: retirees, small businessmen, small savers. I really wanted to heal the damage I'd done, at least in part.

The time to present Counselor Guido Barillo with the check had come. He'd been in charge of the Savings Bank during my time there. He's a very powerful man, he's spent a lifetime on the boards of directors of the largest banks in Italy. He's never once been out of the halls of power. It is safe to say that he's one of the key figures in the system.

I was able to put my plan for revenge into effect thanks to a lucky hunch I had had when I was still working there. During a party the bank threw, I met our head of IT, Roberto Giorgetti. He was my age and in his field he was considered a genius. We started dating. I immediately noticed that my colleague completely lost his head after just a few glasses of wine. When he got drunk he seemed to go into a trance, as if he'd been hypnotized. I've never in my life seen anyone else get drunk so easily. Once the drunkeness was over, he wouldn't remember a thing.

One Saturday night I invited him over for dinner. Roberto drank too much wine and after a while he lost control. We started kidding around about our bosses, the way colleagues often do. We traded anecdotes, obsessions, rumors whispered in the hallway, secrets, shortcomings, gossip of all kinds. At a certain point, Roberto started talking about the big boss, our managing director, Counselor Guido Barillo.

"Computer systems are just like human beings. None are perfect, none are flawless."

"And what's our boss's flaw?" I asked.

"Barillo has a weakness for transsexuals"

"That's just gossip," I replied.

"No, it's the truth."

"I don't believe you."

If there's one thing Roberto can't stand, whether he's drunk or sober, it's to have what he says questioned. In any competition, he always wants to have the last word. In the end, he pulled out his ace. He asked to use my laptop, he went online, and after a few seconds we were in Guido Barillo's email account. I couldn't believe my eyes.

We spent an hour digging through his secrets. His thing for transsexuals was a genuine, full-blown obsession. There were lots and lots of photographs depicting him in quite compromising poses. We had a few good laughs. Afterward, I called a taxi and sent Roberto home. The truth is, he really wasn't my type. Spending the night with a man who's drunk isn't my idea of fun. I'm very romantic and romanticism demands a clear head. I was about to say: romanticism demands sincerity. My idea of love has remained the same. I've never updated it.

The next day I realized that Roberto had forgotten to log out of our managing director's account. After a moment's hesitation, and after a short ethical debate with myself on the sanctity of privacy, I decided to remain in our boss's virtual company. I spent Sunday morning snooping. Then it occurred to me it might be worthwhile copying all the material. I said to myself, "You never know, someday it might turn out to be useful." And I was right, that's for sure.

When I decided to take my revenge on Counselor Barillo

and force him to reimburse the savers he'd defrauded, I started studying all the emails that I'd saved. I discovered lots of flaws in the system. His weakness for transsexuals aside, the lawyer also had his superstitions about, for instance, the color red.

I found an email dating from December 31 in which he reckoned with the year that was about to end and told of his hopes for the one to come. He talked about the color red and said that it upset him deeply. A cursed color. Topping the list of his fears was blood, which was why he was a vegetarian. He was afraid of dying of a heart attack. Why? The color of the heart. He didn't like red flowers and he never drank red wine.

I decided to put my plan into action one Saturday morning. Counselor Barillo was in the habit of having an espresso in a very nice café on Via Garibaldi. That day I dressed in red. I wanted to play all the cards I had at my disposal.

As soon as he left the café, I went over to him. He glared at me, obviously very annoyed.

"Go away!"

"Give me your hand."

"Go away!" he insisted.

"I'm very good at telling the future."

"For the last time, go away or I'll call the police."

"Are you afraid of me because I'm dressed in red?"

"Go away."

"I know everything about you."

"Don't talk nonsense."

"Don't you believe me, Counselor Barillo?"

"Have we met?"

"I know you very well, counselor."

As I uttered that last sentence, I almost let a laugh escape me. I made a tremendous effort to choke it back. I was reminded of that scene in the movie *My Friends,* when they make fun of a poor widower at a cemetery. As the man is stand-ing at his wife's grave in somber meditation, one of the friends sets in motion a diabolical trick, a magnificent prank. He persuades the man that he was his deceased wife's lover. A masterful performance. The widower falls for it like a fly tumbling into a honey jar and starts destroying his wife's grave, insulting her with the vilest words imaginable.

"How do you know my name?"

"Haven't you figured out yet that I'm a clairvoyant?"

The lawyer was left speechless. At that point I went over and looked him straight in the eyes. I explained to him that I was a gypsy woman with supernatural powers. I could very easily do him harm but I could also help him. Slowly, he calmed down and started to listen to me. I sensed that the moment to announce the great prophecy had come: "A fire is about to come, a great red fire. Don't fight it. Let it pass," I said in a strong, decisive voice. As I was turning to leave, he slipped a twenty-euro note into my pocket. Not bad for a performance that had lasted a few minutes. This was the first time I'd earned that much since I'd started doing *drabarimos*. To tell the truth, this first encounter was meant to unsettle him. If I wanted my vendetta, or perhaps I should call it a prank, to work, it was better for the prey not to be very clear-minded. The success of a prank doesn't depend only on the bravura of the performance; it's also very important that the prey be distracted.

That same evening, alone in my trailer, I pulled out my laptop and, without wasting too much time, sent a nice email to Guido Barillo. My thoughts were pretty clear. The time to pay the bill had finally come.

Dear Counselor Barillo,

We're an organization that represents the small savers who've been defrauded. We believe that you and your fellow managers were directly responsible for an act of fraud.

We are in possession of material that could destroy your reputation. Attached, please find a couple of photographs that you might take a look at. Think of the consequences of the ensuing blaze: How will your family members react, your wife first and foremost? What would happen if this material were to be published? What would become of your future?

We believe, moreover, that using the salary and retirement bonuses you accrued while you were employed as managing director to reimburse the small savers you did so much to defraud is the right thing to do. You didn't deserve to profit the way you did. We believe that this is the correct solution. It's up to you to solve the problem.

You have three days to comply with our demands.

Otherwise we'll be forced to take action.

Sincere regards.

On the third day, Counselor Barillo held a press conference where he announced that he would be giving back all the money he'd been paid by my ex-bank. Moreover, he insisted on the creation of a fund to pay back the small savers. The press made a big deal of the news. Counselor Barillo had never gotten so much play on the front page.

A few days later, something incredible happened. The public fell head over heels for Guido Barillo, who had suddenly become a moral symbol, a healthy example of an ethical economy, the very model of a respectable banker. He was invited to meet with both the Pope and the President of the Italian Republic. His name began to come up when people wondered who would be the next minister of the economy, or European Commissioner, or governor of the Bank of Italy. Luckily, none of those things never happened. So I wasn't forced to intervene a second time to "dot my *i*'s." All I needed was to see Guido Barillo installed as governor of the Bank of Italy. That would have been the height of absurdity, the prank to end all pranks.

* * *

At last, a piece of good news. Today the doctor told me that tomorrow I can leave the hospital. I can't wait to get out. I miss fresh air and sunshine. He explained that I'll no longer have fingerprints. The damage to my fingers is irreversible. Patrizia no longer exists. She's dead. That means everything makes sense and we've come full circle. The prophecy of Granny Mavus, the real gypsy woman, has come true. "My daughter, you will die soon. Your death will be a brief winter, without cold, without rain, but with heat and fire."

Now I find myself with two options: I can continue my life as a gypsy woman or I can go back to being Patrizia Pascali. I'm in no hurry. There's time to give the matter some serious thought. The important thing is to come to a good decision. My mission—reimbursing the savers—has been accomplished.

That afternoon, Luciano comes to see me. He tells me that his friend, the journalist Laganà, wants to interview me. I tell him that I'm not up to it. I don't want too much exposure. I prefer to remain in the shadows, where there's more room to maneuver. It's true that it's now practically impossible to see anything of Patrizia in me, but still, it's wiser to take all possible precautions. You never know. All it would take is some minor detail to blow my cover. I don't want any nasty surprises.

"You're turning into a star," Luciano says.

"Too much light is bad for the eyes," I reply with a smile.

"You're a heroine."

"Let's not exaggerate."

"You could have a great career."

"No thanks."

Bene vixit qui bene latuit, to live well is to live well concealed. Luciano informs me that a petition signed by prominent political and public figures has been submitted to the

President of the Italian Republic asking him to give me Italian citizenship, since I'm a stateless person, in recognition of the heroic action I performed by braving the flames in order to rescue little Demir. The city of Turin has also taken steps to put me on the list for public housing. The mayor of the city wants to meet with me; no doubt there will be plenty of television cameras. I don't understand this groundswell of generosity and interest. Perhaps a sense of guilt, that might be one explanation. We are a Catholic country, at least officially.

Luciano tells me about the young girl, Virginia, who made up the story about the rape. Why wrongly accuse the Roma? He tells me a story that's part comedy and part tragedy: a young Italian girl, in fact, *italianissima*, "forced" to remain pure until her wedding day to satisfy her grandmother. Luciano always keeps spectacle and theater in mind. Real life abounds in great material.

"I'm thinking about putting together a play based on these events."

"That wouldn't be bad."

"I even have a great title."

"What is it?"

"That's a secret."

"Come on."

"Speaking of secrets, I've got one for you. I'm perfectly serious, Drabarimos."

"So am I, Luciano, I have one, too. You go first."

"I'm a Rom just like you."

"And I'm not a Rom at all."

"Are you serious?"

"Yes."

We spend a lot of time in the hospital corridor telling each other our stories and our respective secrets. The nurses stop noticing our presence. Our stories are long, they require plenty of pauses. Between one secret and another, between one story and another, between one detail and another, between one memory and another, we stop to refresh ourselves with passionate kisses, unlike any we've ever tasted.

CHAPTER THIRTEEN
No one wants to grow

I drive my mother to the airport. Tania insists on coming with us. My mother deeply appreciates the gesture. She makes her sit in back beside her. During the trip they talk and talk. I limit myself to listening. I don't want to disturb this lovely feminine harmony. What are they saying to each other? My mother explains to her that the Calabrian dialect of Cosenza is a beautiful language. It's not true that it's hard to learn. She just needs to come spend a month with her. That's the offer. Tania is very interested. I have a hard time imagining the beautiful blonde struggling with the Calabrian dialect. I have to admit that Tania lacks neither determination nor tenacity. She's a girl with enormous potential. My mother teaches her many Calabrian proverbs: *I guai da pignata i sapi a cucinara chi i gira*, the pot's troubles are familiar to the wooden spoon that stirs it. *Cu pecura si faci, u lupu sa mangia,* he who becomes a sheep will be eaten by the wolf. *Na nuci ndo saccu non scrusci*, a walnut in the sack makes no noise.

My two woman spend a lot of time talking about cooking, especially pastries. My mother boasts of her gifts as a cook. I have to admit she's very good. She's had years to test and perfect recipes of all kinds. That's one of the advantages of being a housewife.

"What's the secret to being a good cook?" asks Tania, like an eager middle-school student.

"Always try," my mamma replies in a very professional tone.

"Good advice."

"And don't be afraid to make mistakes."

"That's the same thing they taught us in our management courses," says Tania with a laugh.

"Pay no attention to critics and keep heading straight down your path," my mamma insists.

"Magnificent," Tania comments.

Tania invites my mother to come visit Finland. Mrs. I Do thanks her, even though now that my grandmother's sick it won't be easy to travel. But you never know. Then they whisper into each other's ears. I imagine all kinds of secrets.

Something tells me that all this whispering serves only one purpose: to bust the chops of yours truly. What can I do, I'm curious, too curious by nature. I pretend to keep my eyes on the road and to focus on driving. But that damn whispering continues, this time accompanied by giggles. I can't bear to stay silent, so I finally decide to remind them of my presence.

"What are you talking about?" I ask, camouflaging my male intrusion with a smile.

"None of your business," replies Mrs. I Do.

"I'm in perfect agreement with your mamma," Tania says approvingly.

"All right then. I'll shut up," I say brusquely.

As you can see, I followed my mother's advice to the letter: Always try. Moreover, I pay no attention to the criticism leveled at my inopportune intrusion. I take it philosophically. Why take offense? Being kept out of a game is hardly the end of the world.

We get to the airport early, the way Mrs. I Do likes it when she travels. I think she must be predisposed to military order. She could have enjoyed a successful career in the army and become a general. Unfortunately members of the weaker sex (that's another saying that pisses me off) were only admitted into the barracks a few years ago. If there's one thing that my mother hates, it's showing up late. For her, punctuality is everything:

respect, manners, reliability, and so on. On this point we're completely different. In my life as a traveler I've been late lots and lots of times. A number of times I've missed flights, and had to eat the price of the ticket. Now that I think about it, my mother would fit in perfectly well in Finland and other Nordic countries where organization is a basic principle of daily life. There was a terrible mistake: She shouldn't have been born in the northern Mediterranean, that is, in southern Italy, but in northern Europe.

When the time comes to say goodbye and exchange final pieces of advice, Tania sinks into a long hug with my mamma. To hell with all that Nordic formality. The integration of the lovely blonde into the Mediterranean world is going famously. My mamma returns the hug, with lots of kisses.

On the way back from the airport, Tania praises my mamma at great length. She's fascinated by her personality, and especially by her strength of character. In other words, a real woman, very courageous. Who can say otherwise? It's a sentiment I can only endorse. It's quite true that every once in a while she drives me crazy, she treats me like a private in the army, but deep down she's a woman with exceptional qualities. That's something I've always recognized. Of course I can't be objective, but the truth is clear and there is no need for evidence or demonstrations. We can say it loud and clear: Enzo Laganà has the sharpest mother on earth. On this particular point, there is no right of rebuttal. Full stop. Conversation over.

* * *

In the afternoon I drop by Giacomo's café. At a certain point, I see the cousin of the good little virgin come in, Giuliano (I have an exceptionally good memory for people's names). He wants to talk to me. What about? No idea. Now I've built up quite an immunity against lies, hoaxes, and pranks.

We sit down in a secluded corner. I see that he's a little hesitant about where to begin. I encourage him to come out into the open. I don't have time to waste. I'm sick and tired of the whole story of the good little virgin and of virginity itself, God rest its soul.

"Well, what do you want to tell me?"

"I don't know where to begin."

"Well, for example, you could start with your cousin the liar."

"Virginia isn't a liar," he insists.

"You're right. She's worse than a liar."

"That's not true," he continues to insist.

"So what do you call what she did?"

"Virginia isn't the only one responsible."

"Why don't you just spill the beans?" I say, starting to lose what little patience I have. If this keeps up, I'm going to tell him to go to hell right quick. Enough is enough.

"It was me," he says.

"It was you, what?"

"It was me who had sex with her."

"You deflowered your cousin?"

"Yes."

"Why didn't you say so right away?"

"We were afraid."

"Afraid of who?"

What we need here is a priest and a confessional, at the very least. Instead we're going to have to make do with a reporter on the crime beat. We are in the presence of a plot twist. At last we know who deflowered the good little virgin. Mystery cleared up. Hooray! The story can be titled *The Good Little Virgin and the Budding Young Stallion* or else *The Little Lamb and the Young Shepherd*. The behind-the-scenes machinations and the details are excellent ingredients for a slice-of-life story, a goddamned two-bit scoop, or else a movie, erotic but also comic. Only comedy can save us.

The two Ferreri cousins are (or perhaps we should say *were*) practically siblings. They grew up together. Then nature got the better of them. In short, nothing to be done about it, it's stronger than culture, tradition, or grandmothers. They started dabbling in erotic play and experimenting sexually. At a certain point they went a little too far and lost control entirely. The day of the great prank, that is, the fake rape, they saw each other at the grandmother's apartment. It all happened right under her nose. In the blink of an eye, her virginity, the grandmother's treasure, the family jewel, was gone.

"Whose idea was it to drag the two Roma twins into it?" I ask him.

"Virginia's. I swear it."

"And you went along with it like an asshole," I add.

"We had no choice."

"Stop talking bullshit."

The young man starts crying. It's clear that he's spent days brooding over this. His sense of guilt is very strong. Feeling guilty seems to me like the very least he can do. There's a bill to be paid. There always is. Still, there's one thing that remains unclear to me. I thought that he was upset about the consequences of their prank, the drama of the fake rape, but it turns out I was wrong. What worries him most isn't the fate of the Roma, but something else entirely.

"Can I ask you a favor?" he asks me in a sad voice.

"Go right ahead."

"Keep everything we've said here to yourself."

"Oh, really? And why would you ask me to maintain professional confidentiality?"

"We don't want our families to know."

"Especially not your grandmother."

"She'd never forgive us."

"That would be a tremendous tragedy," I add in an ironic tone, very theatrically.

"Our grandmother, as you know, is very old and has lots of health problems."

"This could be the kiss of death."

I feel like giving him a swift kick in the ass. Or at least like letting off some verbal steam. I could clarify one or two things by telling him: "You know what I say to you, my budding young stallion? I don't give a fuck about your family, your grand-mother, and least of all about your cousin's virginity." Lord above, enough is enough. This type of situation annoys the hell out of me. I can't stand hypocrisy. Showing all the good things to the outside world and hiding all the bad things. Another thing that pisses me off is this tendency people have to get away with things and never pay the price. I'm sorry, dear cousin stal-lion, you're not going to be able to escape your responsibilities. You need a good, hard lesson to help you grow. Maybe some-day you'll thank me. Now is the time to learn.

"Why did you tell me this new version?"

"It's not a new version, it's the truth," he insists.

"Let's say it is the truth. Why come to me?"

"Because you're a respectable person. We deceived you before."

"I think it's for some other reason," I say, pushing him up against the ropes.

"What do you mean?"

"Come on, Giuliano, show me your cards," I put in.

"I don't have any cards."

"Then I'll play your hand for you, all right? You're cover-ing for your cousin."

"I don't understand."

"Virginia alias the Good Little Virgin is an underage call girl."

It's time to play my ace. I dust off the reporting done by Silvana, the clever intern, on young female prostitutes in Turin. I add a bit of nonsense, pile the bullshit up here and there, to

make sure it all cooks up into a nice stew. I'm absolutely unin-
terested in the quality and the contents. In cases like this one,
what takes precedence is abundance, sheer quantity, and style
above all. Giuliano slowly comes out into the open and starts
to play the game. He admits that he's heard this rumor about
his cousin. But he swears that it has nothing to do with her. It's
all lies, nothing more.

Giuliano realizes that it's not going to be easy to convince
me. If someone's lied once, they might lie again. I'm reminded
of one of Nietzsche's great quotes (he lost his mind right here
in Turin, during a stay that lasted several months). I don't
remember the exact words, but the point was something along
the lines of: I'm not mad because you lied to me, but because
from now on, I won't ever trust you again. Isn't that so great?
Giuliano doesn't give up, he gives it his all to make me believe
he's telling the truth. Finally he decides to play his own ace. He
pulls his ID out of his jacket and shows it to me.

"Look carefully at the date of birth."

"March 21, 1992."

"Doesn't that tell you anything?"

"The start of spring," I throw out.

"Yes, but it's also the day this whole mess began."

"Enough with this fucking game. Show me your cards!" I
explode. By now my reservoir of patience has been exhausted.

"Virginia gave me a present for my eighteenth birthday.
Now do you understand?"

"Certainly. Not a bad present, eh? Tell me something, what
time were you born?"

"At dawn."

"Then you're really screwed," I conclude.

I sincerely enjoy explaining a few things to him. The famous
sex act or fake rape took place in the afternoon. Therefore, at
the moment of the sex act he was no longer a minor. But his
cousin still was. The law is very clear on this point. For an adult

to have sex with a minor is a crime. And if you're found guilty of this crime, you go to prison. To be perfectly frank, I'm not especially well informed on legal matters. But that doesn't matter; I'm not talking to a judge, or a lawyer, or an expert in the field. The most important thing now is to give a good performance, to be totally convincing. I have a small goal I'd like to accomplish, and I believe it's within reach.

"What should we do?" he asks me, very worried.

"Everything you can to avoid going to jail."

"Which means what?"

"Tell the whole story."

"To who?"

"To everyone. Not just to your grandmother. Do you understand?"

"You want us to do an interview?"

"Unfortunately, that isn't enough. You're going to have to turn yourselves in to the police."

"Oh, sweet Jesus!"

"I don't see any other way, Giuliano."

The boy starts crying again. He's terrified of prison. Now he's not worrying anymore about what his grandmother might say.

I decide not to force the hand. I try to calm him down. There is a very strong likelihood that he's not going to wind up in prison. First of all, there are the standard mitigating factors that no defendant is denied (all you have to have is a lawyer who's a real son of a bitch), then there's the fact that people who turn themselves in are given special treatment, and, last of all, the sexual relationship with his cousin, that is, the good little virgin, was consensual. This wasn't a rape. I add another very reasonable consideration: If the judge they get assigned, male or female, has a weakness for romantic stories, then the chances of an acquittal only increase because the judge will give a certain weight to that aspect of the story, to the idea of

Virginia giving her virginity as a birthday present. That's all very poetic and sentimental, isn't it? In other words, even judges have been in love at least once in their loves. And often your first love, the one you never forget, dates back to your adolescence. We've all been there.

In the end, he accepts my advice. Actually, it's not really advice at all; it's blackmail. Either he does what I tell him, or I'll pillory him in public. He has no alternative. His back's against the wall. We come to an agreement on a few minor matters. Immediately after turning himself in, he's going to give an interview, to my newspaper of course, and he's going to tell the truth, the whole truth, as well as apologize sincerely to the Roma. I'll let Silvana, the intern, do the interview.

Giuliano promises me that he'll do all he can to persuade the family to close the door on this unpleasant story as soon as possible. We'll see if he has any luck. Otherwise, I'll lose my temper and that'll just be too bad for him, for his pretty little virgin, for their grandmother, and for the whole Ferreri family.

* * *

That evening we pack our bags. Tomorrow morning, at last, we're leaving for our holiday in the mountains. Tania's very happy. I, too, can't wait to get away from it all and spend a few days in peace and tranquility. I leave it to Tania to pack the suitcases. She's a first-rate packer. She can boast of extensive experience as a traveler. I sit down in the living room to savor an ice-cold Peroni. My moment of calm doesn't last long. My cell phone rings. It's Maritani. What does he want? Maybe he's going to ask me again to act as a witness in his defense, to rescue him from the editor in chief's wrath.

"Enzo, something incredible's happened."

"Let's hope it's something good."

"Salvini apologized to me."

"Come on!"

"I swear it."

"I can't believe it."

This is certainly a spectacular plot twist. Salvini apologizing constitutes a genuine scoop. So miracles do exist! Maritani reveals the behind-the-scenes details. The public response to the good little virgin's confession was very positive. The editor in chief (not poor Maritani) was praised left and right for his ethical stance. Of course, he's going to be the guest of honor tonight on *Rear Window*, Italy's most popular TV talk show. Our newspaper is going to win some prize or other. There's no doubt about it. Maritani is very happy. To me, it's the umpteenth demonstration that there's no fixing this world we live in. There's no point even trying to reform it, we just need to throw it away and rebuild it. That's right, it would take a revolution. The problem though is that every fucking revolution brings with it a fucking counterrevolution, that is, its own death. And so? I'm starting to get a headache. I give up. I need some rest. At this point, I'm just raving.

ACKNOWLEDGMENTS

I'd like to thank Irene Agnello, Chiara Carrer, Daniele Castellani Pirelli, Claudio Ceciarelli, Mirella and Roberto De Angelis, Sandro Ferri, Massimiliano Fiorucci, Stefano Galieni, Armando Gnisci, Elise Gruau, Christine Love, Robert Love, Stephanie Love, Massimiliano Malato, Federica Mazzara, Grazia Nigro, Sandra Ozzola, Annalisa Pallotti, Serenella Pirotta, Emanuele Ragnisco, Claudio Rossi, Grace Russo Bullaro, Gabriele Santoro, Patrizia Storelli Felten, and all my friends at E/O. I'm very grateful to my friend Marco Cena, who shared with me a number of memories of his family history as a Piedmontese Sinti.

Amara Lakhous was born in Algiers in 1970. He has a degree in philosophy from the University of Algiers and another in cultural anthropology from the University la Sapienza, Rome. *Clash of Civilizations Over an Elevator in Piazza Vittorio* (Europa Editions, 2008) was awarded Italy's prestigious Flaiano Prize and was described by the *Seattle Times* as a "wonderfully offbeat novel."